MW00939886

Facing
Death

Catyana Skory Falsetti

All rights reserved. No part of this publication may be reproduced, distributed, or transmitted in any form or by any means, including photocopying, recording, or other electronic or mechanical methods, without the prior written permission of the publisher, except in the case of brief quotations embodied in critical reviews and certain other noncommercial uses permitted by copyright law. For permission requests, write to the publisher, at cat@catyanaskoryfalsetti.com.

Copyright © 2016 Falsetti Publishing

All rights reserved.

ISBN:-10 1530690927
ISBN-13: 978-1530690923

DEDICATION

Dedicated to my wonderful husband, Tony.
My partner, my muse and the love of my life.

This is a work of fiction. Names, characters, businesses, events and incidents are either the products of the author's imagination or used in a fictitious manner. Any resemblance to actual persons, living or dead, or actual events is purely coincidental.

ACKNOWLEDGMENTS

I want to thank everyone who has helped me through my career, in particular Captain James Carr, Captain Fernando Gajate, Inv. Wendy Crane, Dr. Carolyn Revercomb and many others. Many thanks to my mother Olivia Skory, for her encouragement, and those who have guided and believed in me as well: Nancy White and David Skory. I am grateful to my many friends, who have believed in me.

CHAPTER 1

Roanoke, Virginia

April 2002

I grasp both eyeballs in my right hand. The smooth, round wooden orbs weigh heavily in my palm and I stare into the dark and empty eyes sockets of the dead man's skull.

I set the prosthetic eyes down and examine the cranium. It is a light-brown eggshell color, with a smooth but porous texture, much like a thick seashell. I run my fingers down the zygomatic arch—the cheekbone of the skull—to get a sense of the shape of the face I was determined to create.

It is my job to give this man his face back, or at least a close approximation to what he looked like during life. Hopefully give him enough of a resemblance so that someone who knew him will be able to identify him. He is the most recent unidentified person who was found off Interstate 81 near Roanoke, Virginia. When his body was discovered it was so decomposed that it was unrecognizable and no personal identification such as a wallet or jewelry was found. After several weeks of trying to identify him through missing person notices, the police called me in to help.

My usual duty station is located at the northern office of Virginia's Office of the Chief Medical Examiner, in Fairfax, just ten miles outside Washington, D.C. I am here because I was called to create a facial reconstruction for our south western office in Roanoke, which is approximately four hours from my home near the northern office and deep in the heart of mountain country; centered west of the Blue Ridge and east of the Alleghany's.

I am twenty-seven years old and working at my first, full-time professional forensic science job: "Julia T. Rawson, Forensic Death Investigator." I work as the information collector for the doctors to help them determine the cause and manner of death. My major research paper for my Master's Degree in Forensic Sciences focused on the scientific studies supporting the use of facial reconstruction in law enforcement and being a lifelong artist I understood the sculpture aspect, and was happy to learn more of the science behind the process.

I've always wanted to use my artistic skills to help people, and this seemed the perfect way to do so. I'm lucky to have a great boss, Dr. Catherine Reeves, who was willing to loan me out to our sister agency. She is an outstanding pathologist, scholar and supportive supervisor who believes in the use of forensic art and my abilities.

I sit in a spare laboratory room within the medical examiner's office with off-white walls and faded blue cabinets lined up like school lockers. I rotate on my swivel chair and open the reports sitting next to me, reveling in the peace and relative quiet of the room. The file I've been provided includes a stack of papers with police, anthropology and pathology reports.

The remains of the man whose skull sits in front of me were discovered two months ago in a wooded area. According to the crime scene report, his body was found when a dog got loose from his owner, who stopped at a rest area. The proud canine presented his newly-found treasure to his master, a shoe that happened to still have a human foot inside. The dog owner contacted the police with her story and that ignited a police search, and then the ultimate discovery of the rest of the body.

The rest of the body was hidden from view under an oak tree, partially buried several meters behind the rest stop off of highway Route 81. This road courses for quite a distance, beginning at the US/Canada border in New York state and weaves southwest through Virginia, terminating in Knoxville, Tennessee meandering in and out of the wooded hills through remote areas and small southern towns. The pathologist's report states that the decedent is likely in his sixties and notes stab marks found on the decomposing skin of his abdomen: ruled a homicide. Due to where he was found, off of a major throughway, we can only assume that the man could be from anywhere - and the same likely holds true for his killer.

I attach the mandible to the inferior portion of the temporal bone with a brand of glue called Duco Cement, using a bit of cotton to act as a spacer, imitating the soft tissue that would have been in between the bones during life. This type of glue is used because it holds well but can be easily removed with a bit of acetone, with no damage done to the skull. The cotton helps the jaw settle into a more natural position.

While waiting for the glue to dry, I flip through the various photographs provided in the case file. The first one shows a small brick building that is denoted as the rest stop, with graceful arches reminiscent of a grander time with naked trees surrounding it and the tips of the mountain slopes in the distance. He was found in February so the trees were still bare. The next image shows a rainbow of brown grasses, tramped down into a path where the body was found. The next images are of the surrounding wooded area, which according to the crime scene diagram was over one hundred feet behind the rest stop building behind a large tree. The side of the hill is brown with tangled bushes where his body was found, and a black plastic bag peeking up from under some brush. I pull the picture closer to me to examine the close-ups that detail the decedent's face, mostly decomposed. The tip of the wrinkled nose cartilage shows a slight upward tilt at the end. The shape of the cartilage is something that the skull cannot tell me, so this information helps me to understand his nose shape. From the decomposition and the wear of the fabric of his clothes, it looks like he was there for a while.

The crime scene photos followed all of the steps that I was taught in school — an overall, mid-distance and close up shots of the scene that visually tell a clear story. I don't take this for granted, as from what I have seen from other scenes often times there is not always a trained photographer available.

The main door clicks open and Adam Conner, the death investigator for this office, comes into the room. "This was my case."

I slide out a photograph of the clothing from the pile of pictures. The image shows a blue T-shirt and jeans are tattered and worn with the bones and flesh still in them.

I look up at Adam. "Do you know the size of his clothes?" I flip to the next image. "Oh, wait— here's a photo of the clothing sizes, very good."

Adam pulls a sheet of paper from the pile and points to a line in the police report. "It says here the shirt is a medium and the jeans are thirty-six waist and thirty-two inseam."

I verify the information in the photographs in front of me. "Great, thanks."

Clothing size is the only way to approximate the size of a skeletonized body from decomposed remains. A person can always wear bigger clothes but generally not smaller, so it gives me an idea of the person's build. In this case the remains weighed 110 pounds when he was brought in, but that is a lot less than what he must have weighed in life. He was already so decomposed that a lot of him had melted away. Most of the human body is made of water, so when that goes away the weight loss can be surprising and quick. In life he may have weighed somewhere in the 170s, judging by the size of his clothing.

A large man with spiky red hair ambles into the room he has an imposing-looking camera hanging around his neck and carrying a large nylon bag and a tripod in his meaty hands. "Hey." He nods to Adam then walks over to me; his hair doesn't seem to move at all with the hair spray coating that is holding it. "So you are the artist." A statement.

"That's me." I agree. "I am guessing you are the photographer." I give him a crooked smile.

"Yup - Brian." He extends his thick fingers and we shake hands. His palm is dry and rough. "Dr. Marcosi asked me to take some photographs of the skull and the reconstruction process."

I'm impressed – my office doesn't have a dedicated photographer so many of us have learned to take our own pictures. Having good photographs taken by a trained expert is essential to a successful facial reconstruction, especially valuable in order to create a 2-D reconstruction, or a drawing based on the skull. Bad photos, lens distortion and skewed angles can really confuse the accuracy of the image.

"Great. I will need frontal and lateral photographs to scale. The more you can take, the better for documenting everything. I like having pictures of the skull at all possible angles when I'm working on the sculpture."

Brian gently sets down his camera on an adjacent table and pulls out a contraption that unfolds into an umbrella for deflecting light, a gray card to test the lighting, a macro and micro lenses, and a reflector. He is a serious photographer.

I hear the door open behind me and a man wearing light-blue scrubs walks in. Adam looks up. "Oh, Dr. Marcosi, this is Julia, the forensic artist from Fairfax."

I look up and am surprised to see how short and squat the Chief doctor of this office appears. His body shape reminds me of a Weeble, a roly-poly toy from childhood. *"Weebles wobble but they don't fall down."* I smile to myself. Dr. Marcosi has a full head of too-black hair—it looks like a toupee or small animal —with knobby hands, one of which he extends to me. The other holds a brown paper bag.

"Hi, thanks for coming down," he says as we shake hands, his grasp is strong and dry. "How is everything working for you?"

"Looking good so far," I answer. Since I am sitting on a stool, our eye level is about the same. "I did have a couple of questions about the hair and the anthropological report. I want to get this reconstruction done as accurately as possible, and I already have so many questions."

He replies, "You can give the anthropologist a call. I think he's still at the number on the report you have. I think your boss worked with him once and has said good things about him. And, I heard you had a question about the hair."

He reaches into the paper bag and pulls out a clump of hair. It is a small accumulation, brown and gray in color, held together by dirt and dried fluid, presumably the hair I saw in the image that had been sent to me.

"Excellent." I put down the skull and reach over to examine the mass. I am glad to see it, as it is helps greatly with the accuracy of the hair when creating a reconstruction. There is no way to tell information about a person's hair from the skull alone. Since hair is so important to how a person looks, I hate to speculate on a color, style, or length.

"It was good to meet you." Dr. Marcosi says. "I hope this helps, I have to get back to work. Thanks again for coming down."

The doctor leaves and Adam follows him. So it is just the photographer, Brian, and me, each focusing on our tasks.

The skull sits on a stand I had made from a pipe screwed into a board. I place the stand, including the skull on a safe part of the counter, nowhere near the edge.

I step back, looking at the set up. "Okay, I need the photographs to be at the Frankfort horizontal position."

"What does that mean?" Brian looks confused.

"It's the natural position that a person holds his head in life. I find it by creating a line from the base of the socket of the orbit to the top of the external auditory meatus, or ear hole." I take out a level and create the imaginary line between the eye and the ear and straighten the skull into the correct position.

I slide out a paper crime scene ruler from my art kit and hold it vertical - parallel next to the skull and position it at the same level as the zygomatic arch so both the skull itself and the numbers on the ruler will be in focus.

"We need to position the camera at eye level to the skull. Or where his eyes would have been. I'll need some photographs printed out to scale so I can make 2-D images, too. I like to do this to help me with the nose shape."

Brian peers at the skull. "I don't know how you do this; all skulls look the same to me."

"Once you have seen a few, the subtleties are easier to spot. The skull is the base architecture for all our faces. So each one is as different as every face on the planet. The head shape and the distance between the central features—eyes, nose, and mouth—are the most important. Those are what make us recognizable during life."

I lean over to touch the mandible to see if the glue has dried. "Thanks for taking the pictures; they'll be really great to refer to, especially when the clay is on and I won't be able to see the skull. I don't want to lose track of the subtleties. It helps me be true to the data it provides."

"How do you know what the nose looks like?" Brian stares into the skull's empty eye sockets.

"There are mathematical formulae that have been established by anatomists and anthropologists to anticipate the length of the nose based on skeletal structures, and there are clues from the shape of the nasal aperture for how the nose looks. But I can't tell for certain what the tip of the nose will be like, bulbous or pointy, so I want to keep it sort of average so it doesn't sway the viewers. My reconstruction isn't going to be an exact portrait, but it will certainly be more recognizable than a skull to put out on the news."

Brian takes some candid shots of me handling the skull, and I turn it to face him. I feel funny doing this, always uncomfortable in the spotlight. Then Brian sets up his camera on a tripod and puts it into position, about six feet away from the subject so there will be no lens distortion. I move in and out to adjust the skull and add and take out the paper scale so we have images with and without it.

When Brian leaves to print out the photographs, I settle into the hard, high-seated lab chair as best as I can and stare at the skull to examine its subtleties. I tear off bits of a cotton ball from a bag I had brought and insert them into the orbits, holding them in place with masking tape.

I had already fashioned eyes from wooden spheres that I'd purchased and painted by hand. They are twenty-five millimeters in diameter, which is the average size for a human eyeball. Having been told that the decedent was of European ancestry, I painted the irises a nondescript hazel with flecks of grey and brown, since I have no idea what color his specific eye color may have been during life. It is important not to give the reconstruction characteristics that we are not certain of, and I want to make a generic image for media use. I know that by examining the features of the skull, the reconstruction can reflect the face shape, and the placement of eyes, nose, and mouth in relation to one another. I also refer to the studies about the length of the nose projection and the width of the mouth, but the distinctive soft tissue features of each cannot yet be determined scientifically. This is where artistic latitude and interpretation comes into play.

I pull out the book, *Forensic Art and Illustration* by Karen T. Taylor, which includes some facial tissue depth measurements gathered by J. S. Rhine and H. R. Campbell in the 1980s. I also take a look at my own research paper from my master's thesis on the subject, since I had collected similar charts from studies done all over the world.

Anatomists and anthropologists have been measuring facial tissue depth since the late 1800's in order to understand the distribution of fat and muscle under the skin. The depths of soft tissue (distance from the bone to the surface of the skin) are grouped into different tables, divided by race and sex. I run my finger down the table to the numbers in the white male group. Then I use digital calipers to measure each tissue depth marker and cut it with a scalpel. I slice them one by one, oh so slowly, for accuracy and then number them. By the time I am done, I have thirty-two erasers lined up in a row, ready to be glued to the skull.

I review the forensic anthropological report again, making sure I read each paragraph closely before calling the anthropologist with the specific questions that I have about the age of the deceased. I look down at the contact information associated with the report. Dr. Michael Cuezze—with a 505 area code.

I glance down at my watch; it is 11:25am here, so only 9:25am in New Mexico. My heart thuds, as I am a bit of an anthropologist groupie. I studied anthropology during my undergraduate studies and had considered getting my Ph.D. in physical anthropology, focusing on forensics, but was discouraged by the lack of job prospects. I think there might be somewhere on the order of eighty practicing board-certified forensic anthropologists in the United States, so I got my Master's Degree in Forensic Sciences, instead.

I dial the phone, and a male voice answers after the second ring. "Michael Cuezze, Osteology Lab." His voice is deep. No "Doctor" in front of it, so not pretentious already. I smile. I explain who I am, that I work at the Medical Examiner's Office in Virginia for Dr. Catherine Reeves.

"Oh yes, I used to work with Catherine here in New Mexico. She was a tremendous asset here at the university and the Office of the Medical Investigator." He has a smooth voice and a comfortable way of speaking that make me relax.

"I'm creating a facial reconstruction based on observations from a case you previously analyzed. I guess they sent him out to you in February. An unidentified white male." I recite the case number to him.

"Hold on, let me look this up." I hear the ticking of a keyboard and then a pause. "Okay, I remember that case."

"I'm wondering if you have any ideas about what age I should make him look like. The range in the report is kind of broad: forty-five to sixty."

"Well, it's hard to tell. People sometimes age well or sometimes not so much." He chuckles.

"That is true."

"But I would make him look around fifty or so, with a hard life, since he was missing all of his teeth and the mandible and maxilla showed signs that the teeth had been absent for some years."

"Thank you." I'm relieved he has given me some guidance. "Do you have any other thoughts about the facial reconstruction?"

"Oh wow, I don't know. I never really think too seriously about what they look like with skin on." He chuckles again. "You should talk to Stan Rhine; he's the one who developed all those tissue depth measurements you folks use."

Stan Rhine—*wow!* I know that name well. His research papers were a major contributor to my master's thesis. Dr. Rhine performed the first modern facial tissue depth studies in the 1980s. Before him, the only tissue depth measurement data was from the 1890s. From that time on there were historical reconstructions done, but it wasn't until the 1960s that the skill was used for forensic purposes. In 1967 Betty Pat. Gatliff, a medical illustrator, and Dr. Clyde Snow, an anthropologist, worked together to create a facial reconstruction of an unidentified decedent found in Oklahoma. She created a clay sculpture from the skull, using the tissue depth data from the 1890s, and the sculpture came out accurately. Her results were enough to stimulate a lead that resulted in a positive identification, and ultimately providing some closure for the family.

There was a need for more-current data on faces of different ethnic groups and ages and Dr. Stan Rhine took on the project. Because he worked at the anatomy lab with the Medical Examiner at the University of New Mexico, he had cadavers to use to do the study. To get tissue depth measurements, he took a needle and inserted it into the skin at twenty-one points and then measured each depth. He added up and averaged the numbers for each of the 21 points, and these are what artists now use to make a reconstruction. He did this with two distinct racial groups: American whites and American blacks. His study was revolutionary in the field, and I felt excited to learn that he was still around and working. I would love to meet him one day. "Please tell Dr. Rhine how much I, and many others, appreciate his work."

Michael laughs, low and inviting. "I'll definitely let him know. He's a great guy, very open and professorial."

"Thank you for taking the time to talk to me. Can I e-mail you if I have any more questions?" I'm feeling warmth through my body and want to stay on the phone, but I don't want to be pushy.

"Anytime. I'm always happy to help. I would love to hear if the person is identified, we almost never get any direct feedback on our skeletal estimates."

"Thank you so much. I will definitely let you know. Have a great day." I hang up the phone and pause, imagining what he looks like, dark and handsome for sure . . . I would like to meet him one day. I realize that I've heard his name before. When

I was looking into getting my Ph.D. years ago, I'd heard that the University of New Mexico had a good program. I was told it was because of a certain anthropologist, and then it dawns on me that anthropologist was Dr. Cuezze.

For a moment I let my thoughts stray to what it would have been like if I had pursued my Ph.D. in anthropology and wonder where that would have led. Then I shake my head back to the present.

Adam enters the room holding a paper bag.

"More hair?" I ask.

He laughs. "No, I got some sandwiches for us from the local diner. I hope you like turkey." He puts the bag on the counter. "I would join you, but I have an appointment. There is a nice picnic table outside though."

"Thank you, that was nice of you. Turkey sounds great." A good time to take break, and I get up and move to eat outside at the picnic table and enjoy the warm sun on my skin and the fresh air. The medical examiner's office is situated off the main throughway in Roanoke with woods surrounding it, so the outside is actually looking at trees. That's one thing I don't like about working in a laboratory—at least all the ones I have been in so far. No windows, only standard-issue fluorescent light bulbs, so I feel starved for natural light. I scarf down the food and go back to work, getting focused and into a zone. The next step is to glue the markers I cut earlier onto the skull for my reference points.

This step takes time, since each marker has to be placed properly on the accurate anatomical landmark. Tissue depths all refer back to a location on the skull that everyone can agree upon. The scientific method requires repeatability, so the anatomists and anthropologists agreed on names, descriptions, and locations for specific landmarks. Now when they discuss them, everyone knows what they're talking about. Communication is the key.

With the markers securely adhered to the skull, I lean back, my shoulders stiff from being hunched over for so long. Now the glue has to dry. If I touch it too soon, I will mess it up and have to start all over again. I have to stop myself, as I am not the most patient person in the world and like to move quickly and efficiently once I begin a project.

I look up at the clock. It is almost 4:00 and time to call it a day. Perfect timing. The tissue depth measurements will dry overnight and I can get started on the actual reconstruction in the morning.

Adam bursts into the room and announces, "Quitting time."

He looks at the skull—it is sitting on a stand with what looks like blunt spikes coming out of the face. "It looks like something out of a horror movie."

"Yes, I forget how creepy it can appear to the uninitiated." Like the remnants of a torture victim from one of the slasher movies I used to love as a teenager.

"Can I take you to dinner, as a thank you for coming down? I can show you around the huge metropolis of Roanoke." He chuckles.

"Sounds good." I'm always interested in exploring new places, but also worry about being hit on. He is wearing a wedding ring, so I hope he is just being colleague level friendly.

"I'll pick you up at your hotel in an hour," he says as we make our way to the parking lot and go our separate ways.

Back at the hotel, I change into jeans a shirt and sweater, nothing fancy. When Adam picks me up, he says, "Sorry we didn't get a better hotel. I don't know if there really are any here."

He laughs but I don't think he's joking. The tour of Roanoke begins with what he calls the best Mexican restaurant in the area, complete with a decor of brightly painted colors, loud music, and sombreros on the wall that is so common among Mexican restaurants in the U.S. I have been to Mexico and know that it is much more the stereotype than reality.

After dinner he drives me around the small city, situated in the valley. It is made up mostly small, single-family homes, lots of trees, and strip malls, from what I can see.

"Roanoke is relatively small, especially compared to the DC area. There are around ninety thousand people in the area. There isn't much to see, but there is one thing that you should definitely see: Mill Mountain Park," he says and points out the window to a star standing alone on the side of a green-and-brown mountain. "And that's the Roanoke Star. It's been here for as long as I remember, and it's the symbol of Roanoke."

We drive on through the well-lit city streets, past residential cottages that look to have been built in the 1930s. The road gets darker, but in the distance we can still see the brightly lit, man-made star. As we meander uphill, I crack the window to let in the sweet smell of spring, and then sneeze. Oh my allergies. At the top of the road there is a park that is surprisingly filled with people.

"It's busy, I think, because the weather is warmer than it has been in a while," Adam comments. "It was a cold winter for us. Even snowed twice."

I think how lucky we were to have missed the snow in northern Virginia—this year.

Families are milling around, looking over a stonewall barrier to the edge and sitting at picnic tables. Next to the parking lot, there is a lookout point and a little wooden shack where a blackboard leaning against the wall announces that they have ice cream and hot dogs. We park and get out of the car and make our way to the overlook point.

"What a great view," I say. Roanoke spreads out below, a blanket of darkness with the city lights blinking back at us. We stand for a few minutes watching the families. I don't know what else to talk about with him at this point, and I want to have some down time. A wash of exhaustion floods over me. I yawn hugely and quickly cover my mouth with my hand. "Wow, I just got really tired."

"Well, that's a tour of the best of Roanoke in a night," Adam says. "I guess I should get you back so you can get some sleep, to wake up fresh and finish giving this guy a face."

We head back to the car. The drive back is quiet and I feel relieved. Small talk makes me tired.

I'm glad to get back to the hotel and watch some mindless television for a little while, and then pass out on the strange bed.

I don't sleep very well and miss my two cats, Simon and Kudo, cuddling around me. I manage to get up quickly the next morning, as I am energized by my task. This is my first actual facial reconstruction case, and I am excited and nervous all at the same time. I have done so much research and training on the subject but this is the first time I get to really use my skills when it matters. The joy of getting to create feels wonderful and gives me a sense of contributing to something greater than the usual checklist of duties.

Once back at the office, I check the tissue depth markers. The glue has dried, and it looks good except for one marker hanging off, number 19, one of the longest ones situated on the side of the jaw. I add a dollop of glue and push the eraser back onto the skull, holding it for a full minute, hoping that will suffice in getting it to stay on.

I lean back and examine his facial architecture, pondering the subtleties and mentally planning my stylistic approach. Wondering what his life was like—usually people who are found under these circumstances have lived a rough and dangerous life—this is demonstrated by seeing the aging in the wear of his bones and the lack of teeth. Brian comes back and photographs the skull with the markers. He has brought me the prints that he took earlier of the skull with no markers.

Since I am covering the actual skull with clay, I like to have the pictures close by, to keep the details fresh in my mind. Thankfully, Brian returns with a printout of the frontal and lateral sides with the tissue depth markers so I can work on the drawing first. I start a 2D reconstruction by creating a two-dimensional image—or a sketch of the face—rather than jump right into to the clay modeling. I take the photograph of the front of the skull and tape it to a sheet of vellum drawing paper sheet on a board that I brought, then tape a sheet of tracing paper over it. The tissue depth markers serve as a guide for the sketch of a rough image of his face. Due to his estimated age being in the fifties and his lack of natural teeth, I give him droopy eyes and more sunken-in cheeks. The tissue depth markers that I use are from individuals who are much younger, in the mid-twenties, so I keep that in mind, too. People generally lose fat from their face as they age, unless, of course, they gain weight.

My music flows on my headphones and I get lost in the process of the movement of the pencil on the paper, the smooth lines, shading, and the process of birthing an image. After several hours of sketching, I pull out another piece of drawing paper to start the side view. This is an important step, as it is the best way for me to measure the nasal aperture, which indicates the length and direction of his nose. I sway my gaze back and forth from reference materials to the sketch. The width of the nostrils is said to be five millimeters thick on each side of the nasal aperture for a person of European ancestry.

When the sketch is done I examine what I brought together - surprised by the outcome. As I follow the contours of the skull, I clear any preconceived notions in mind—that is my goal—to be led by what I see from the bones. His eyes look out from his long face; he has a comb-over hairstyle, as that is how his mummy looked when it was found. This will give me a good reference when I am working on the skull in clay. The office and the media want a good clay sculpture, as that seems to attract more attention.

I stand up and stretch again feeling the ache. I get so entranced with the process of creation that I forget how long I am sitting in one position. Not so good for my back.

I pull out a block of the oil-based clay from my bag and begin to massage it between my hands to make it softer and easier to manipulate. Brian comes back in every half an hour or so and takes more pictures, getting ones with the eyes in place and then as I start to lay the clay. I place the clay over the face, bringing it to the depth of the tissue depth markers. At this point he looks like a blobby mess.

I start building the nose, squishing the clay between my fingers and rolling them into thin strips for placement. I refer to the formula for the length each piece should be, using the calipers to keep me on track. I also look closely at pictures of the decomposed examining the somewhat decomposed soft tissue of the nose, to help lead the shape.

At every step, I pause to examine my work. Fleshy jowls, heavy eyelids, and a bald face are all I have at the moment. He is starting to look like a human, so that is a good sign. It has been a while since my sculpting class days. An entire day has gone by, and I didn't even notice that it was time to leave the office. I am on my own tonight, to my pleasure, and I stop to get fast food before heading back for a quiet night at the hotel.

The following days fly by in a blur. When I'm working on an artistic project, I get lost in the time and block out everything else around me. I have my CD Walkman and just go where the face leads me while the music keeps me company.

On Wednesday I put the finishing touches on the sculpture before the press conference to be held later in the afternoon. As an artist I never feel I am done with a project. I give him some thin hair, combed over, reflecting the photos of him from the scene and measurements from the hair mass I cleaned.

The press conference is held in the small front room of the building. The conference room, though small, is well appointed and gives no indicators of it being in a morgue, other than the plaque on the wall commemorating the dedication. The panel consists of Dr. Marcosi; Adam, as the lead investigator; and me as the forensic artist. There is also a Virginia State Police trooper who worked the initial scene and who seems curious about this new effort to generate leads on his case.

Only two local television crews and the one newspaper arrive. They take a few minutes to set up their video cameras and microphones. I set up the sculpture with a cloth around his neck to give the illusion of shoulders. The photographers (the newspaperman and Brian) pan and snap pictures at different angles, as well as take photos of the drawing I created, laid out across the table. The media photographers seem to love the sculpture reconstructions, much more than the drawings. It makes the story and image feel more human.

The state trooper and Dr. Marcosi do most of the talking, explaining the circumstance of when the victim was found, and showing off the reconstruction. All in all it takes about thirty minutes. My first experience in person with the press is over almost as soon as it started. Kind of fascinating.

Now it is up to the media to get the image out and in front of the right person—someone who will help identify him by recognizing the face. I keep my fingers crossed and head home after thanking everyone for their hospitality. I choose to drive the four hours back to my home, even though they offered to pay for another night at the hotel. I really want to get back to my own bed.

CHAPTER 2

The next morning, back in Fairfax, driving to my home office, I pull into the parking lot of the Office of the Chief Medical Examiner. I pull up on the parking brake, put the car in gear, and scramble out of my black 1990 Toyota Celica GT and into the fresh April air.

The Medical Examiner's office is located in the ground level of an old brick structure, hidden behind the State Police Barracks and under the Virginia Division of Forensic Science laboratory. An innocuous looking building it is the repository for the stories of the dead, each tale unique, but all with the same ending.

My long, black hair is still damp from my morning shower; the fifteen-minute commute isn't enough time for the hot air from the car's dash vents to dry it. I roll and twirl the length together to secure it to the back of my head with a claw like, black plastic clip. I like to think that I am being ultra-efficient with my time usage as opposed to admitting that I am just too lazy to wake up fifteen minutes earlier in order to use a hair dryer.

I stand and grunt as I pull one bag over my shoulder; I haul two tote bags to work filled with items to always keep me prepared. Pushing the lock button on the door of the car and trying to pull my black suit jacket into place under my coat, I turn and look at how far I have to walk. Not really too far, but it feels like it with these bags.

A black-and-white police car slowly rolls by on its way to the back entrance to the autopsy suite. The officer waves at me and I gesture back, feeling embarrassed that I am not already in the building. That is where I should have been first, before the officers. I sigh in frustration with myself.

The employee parking lot is on the side of the building next to a small, mostly deciduous forest that surrounds on three sides. The official nature of the activities inside this nondescript building makes me feel like I am a part of something bigger than myself.

I trot to the secured entry on the side of the brick building and accidentally drop the bags in front of the door while trying to get my right hand free. I swear under my breath and recover my focus, punching in the security code on the keypad that gives access to the building.

After successfully making my way inside, I move through a small, dark, concrete stairwell and am again required to press more numbers at the final secured entryway. I emerge at the center of the hallway in the main part of the building; it's like being reborn into the bright fluorescent lights. Taking long strides through the shiny gray hall, I breeze past doorways, trying to make it down the corridor to my office before anyone notices I am running late. But they would certainly hear me. My shoes are not the stealth variety and have heavy three-inch heels that clomp like a horse walking down the street. I choose these shoes because they are sturdy, give my stature a lift, and they were on sale.

I make it to my small, shared office at the end of the hall, which is technically at the front of the building from the public's perspective. It's a typical municipal windowless room with gray walls and bland wall-to-wall carpeting, designed purely for function. I slide my way around to the cubby of the heavy, strangely orange-tinted wood desk, and shove my bags under it while glancing over to the adjacent work area. The other desk is partially blocked from view by a four-foot-tall faux-wood bookshelf.

Patrick McConnell, the senior investigator and my office mate, is sitting at his desk. He looks up as I enter. "Good morning, sunshine how was Roanoke?" He smiles. "Eight ten—almost on time." He chuckles, knowing this is my weak spot.

"I know, I know." I drop my bag behind my desk. "Is it busy today?" I unpack my bags and turn on my computer.

"We have a couple of bodies in the back already. I have to make some calls; my wife's doctor." His voice trails off. He rubs his hand over his head, smoothing his short salt-and-pepper hair even more. His wife has been fighting cancer for years.

"No problem. I can handle it." I settle my bags and stand to go. "I'll give you some privacy. See you in the morgue." I leave the carpeted room and head back up the tile hallway.

I move down the cool steel-gray of the hall that leads me to the back of the building, where the energy level is much lower . . . where the dead are waiting. My shoes clip-clop, echoing with every step.

I feel like a mouse in a maze turning to approach the gray double doors that lead into the morgue. Through the first set of doors, I pause in the decontamination area, a small room between the two sets of doors, where my "morgue shoes" wait for me on the floor. I pull off my loud leather shoes and slide on the black-vinyl slip-ons with rubber soles that I bought for this purpose (to keep my regular shoes clean of the gross stuff, or biohazards, resulting from autopsies in the back room). I purchased the cheapest I could find because if they get too tainted, I won't feel bad about chucking them. My professor's voice from graduate school resonates through my mind, reciting Edmond Locard's exchange principle.

In 1910 Dr. Locard started the first crime laboratory in the world, two small rooms in the Paris Police Department. He once stated: "Any action of an individual, and obviously the violent action constituting a crime, cannot occur without leaving a trace."

His original phrasing has since transformed into: "With contact between two items, there will always be an exchange." A person will always transfer trace evidence from item to item, no matter how hard you try not to. That makes me think of how all things in the world are somehow intrinsically connected.

I push through the second set of gray hospital-like doors, entering the autopsy room. The smell hits me first thing. Not exactly a hospital odor, but a special scent all of its own, decomposition mixed with the chemicals that try to wash it away. Everything in sight is a monochromatic wash of light gray-blue color. Gray tiled floors, gray vinyl walls, and steel cabinets and appliances. The entire area has to be washable for decontamination purposes; thus the sterile, easy-clean nature of the equipment.

I pick up a clipboard from the worn wooden desk next to the entrance, the one item that escaped the decontamination policy, and examine the list. Today the office's dead include a suspected (called this until proven) natural death, suicide by hanging, and an accident. Since we don't have any obvious homicides, there are no crime scene investigators present. I can tell the difference between crime scene investigators and other police officers because the CSIs are always in uniform and have little trepidation being with the dead.

There are three stations for autopsies where gross dissections are performed; each has a large sink with a hanging metal scale used to weigh organs over a counter space to dissect them. To finish off the station sits a metal gurney where the bodies lie.

Even the doctors and autopsy technicians blend into the muted surroundings with their light-blue scrubs, worn like protective camouflage. The only people in full color are the police officers sprinkled around the room.

Standing beside two of the doctors are the autopsy technicians, or dieners. *Dieners* is German term for "servant," and has come to mean an assistant to a doctor. Dieners do the heavy lifting and a lot of the major cutting and gross dissection during the autopsy procedure. Our office has only two dieners, and we have three pathologists, so the doctors have to share. Both of our dieners, Doug and Matt, are present today. This is unusual, as one or the other often finds a reason to take off from work.

"Hey Jules! You're back! Glad to see you!" Doug's deep voice reverberates through the tiled space—pulling everyone's attention to me.

"Good morning, Doug," I call back. I feel compelled to respond even though I hate having everyone look at me. Doug laughs then starts to whistle "Stairway to Heaven," which echoes loudly against the tiles.

A group of young men hovers ten feet from the workstation, with an alpha officer leading the pack. I walk by and give them "the nod" that is so common among law enforcement. I get it back from all of them.

I approach Dr. Marko Ivanovic, a Serbian, whom I have found to be a very knowledgeable man but an extremely disorganized and unfocused individual. He epitomizes the stereotype of a mad scientist, with disheveled clothes and unkempt hair. Dr. Ivanovic silently works on a body, bent over and engrossed in something I can't quite see yet.

There is a shortage of qualified pathologists from the United States, so many doctors from all over the world come to work here. Last year only thirty-five doctors passed the forensic pathology board exams, leaving many jurisdictions short of qualified pathologists. That is nowhere near enough to cover all fifty states and over two hundred offices, so many agencies are working with a single certified pathologist acting as chief and overseeing the work of those waiting to take or retake the national certification exam.

The fluorescent lights highlight the ugly pallor over the already unpleasant sight of the naked, overweight, white male lying face down on the steel table.

I hear a male officer murmur from behind me, "He looks asleep." I agree; in this instance the dead guy does look peaceful, just large and naked. The group of five stares with awe and a bit of disgust at the ease and comfort the doctors and autopsy technicians display while moving around and manipulating the dead bodies.

Under the mask I can tell by his eyes that the doctor is smiling as he sees me. "Hey, doc," I chirp. Jeez—I hate how young I sound and remind myself to work on speaking in full and complete sentences.

He nods and gestures. "Julia, look at the lividity," he says in his heavily accented English. It has taken me a bit of practice to be able to understand him, but now my ear is trained. His gloved and bloody hand points at the body's shoulders, where light-colored marks display a lace pattern against the reddish-colored skin. I know it is still human skin, but the texture reminds me of an inflated balloon, taut and smooth.

"Get a picture of this for me, I can use it for my next publication."

Forensic professionals often write papers in order to publish details about findings in interesting cases. This is a good way to get their names out there as well as to help advance the field by sharing findings with others.

The police officers huddle together a few feet away and look around, not knowing where to focus; their eyes drift longingly toward the exit, ready to make a quick getaway. They are positioning themselves as far away from the autopsy tables as they can, in a cluster, avoiding seeing the details of the day's activities, but peeking over knowing they have to in order to complete their reports. I have often found that cops who consider themselves "big and bad"—tough on the street—become quite squeamish around dead bodies.

To get the pictures Dr. Ivanovic requested, I must use the camera that is sitting ready on the metal utility cart that sits next to every station. I remind myself to put on white latex gloves; it is important to use protective covering whenever touching anything in the morgue. The autopsy techs are notorious for using the cameras; push carts, or even the phone while wearing a bloody, gooey glove. So I never know what is covering anything in that room. I learned that the hard way my first week working here, when I grabbed a camera without gloves and got a handful of mystery stickiness. It quickly dawned on me why there are so many sinks in the room. They, along with soap and antibacterial wipes, have become my best friend. And of course, gloves, gloves, gloves.

When ready I wave the cops to come over. Only two approach. "See the pattern of light-colored skin against the red of his back?" I point to the man's back and they nod. "The color difference comes from where the object that was pressing against the skin made a pool, so the negative image of the pattern appears where the blood settled." They look up at me and seem to want more.

I continue my explanation to the small crowd of what I assume to be rookie police officers. "A method of learning information about the circumstances of a person's death is by looking at the pattern of lividity. Lividity, also called livor mortis, is what happens after the heart stops pumping throughout the body. Then, just like water flowing through a pipe, the blood settles in the parts of the body that are closest to the ground. The outlines left by the pooling of the blood show the position of the body at the time of, or right after, death."

"What is this information good for?" a young blond man asks.

I finish snapping the pictures and stand up straight to look at the group again and move the assembly away, leaving the doctor to go back to his work.

"It is especially important when there's a question of the body being moved from where it was discovered. When the marks don't line up with the position, often it is due to the body being moved after the person was dead. That can mean a body was moved after a homicide, but sometimes the body might be moved for another reason."

"Like what?" another man asks.

"We had a case where one guy came in with a suspected heart attack. He was fully clothed, but when we took off his pants he had a ring impression around his bottom and legs from the toilet seat."

One of the viewers' mouths drops open.

"After his wife was questioned further, we found that she had moved him to try to keep his dignity."

The crowd nods.

I move with the group and start an impromptu lecture. "The Medical Examiner's Office in Virginia was one of the first systems in the United States to be transformed from the old coroner system." I look at their faces and they all seem interested. "The word *coroner* is generally thought to have been taken from the word *crowner*, a term used in England in the Middle Ages. During the Medieval period in England they had a crowner, who served as a representative of the king sent out after a death to collect death taxes. Many states like South Carolina still have coroner systems, which are different from the medical examiner system. Unlike a medical examiner, a coroner doesn't have to be a physician, depending on the local requirements, and it's also generally an elected position. I was shocked to learn that in some states the only requirements for office are to be eighteen and have a high school degree, where a medical examiner in Virginia is always a doctor."

"Wow, coroner offices sound scary," one of the officers mumbles.

"I hear that they can be," I agree.

"Interesting," the alpha police officer says. "Well, that's all folks." He gestures and the group starts to move to another table while he looks back at me. "Thanks." I nod back to him.

I try to fill in the gaps for the doctors when communicating with others. I think a reason the police don't like to come in is because they don't like the bodies or the doctors. Pathologists are generally not the most personable people in the world. If someone goes through ten-plus years of medical school to become a pathologist, it's generally not because they have extroverted personalities. A pathologist's salary is a fraction of what other doctors can earn, but there are definitely fewer complaints and lawsuits to deal with in most cases.

Some doctors explain the details and anatomy during the autopsies, but more often than not they simply stare intently at the subject (the dead body) and speak only to the staff, ignoring the police or other bystanders. Some do this because of a lack of understanding or interest on the part of the listener, or some do it as part of an external recitation. Usually the cops just want to know the end result, not how the conclusion was reached.

I refocus on the dead man in front of me. It is a peculiar feeling: being next to the dead. It has taken me several months to get used to being around them, but now, somehow, I have reached a professional level of comfort. As a woman, a rookie, and a person with an ego, I pretended that I was unfazed until it finally became true.

The first time I saw a dead body outside of a funeral was during my internship with the Office of the Chief Medical Examiner in Boston. I was staying there with my husband at the time after graduating with my master's degree. I was looking to get experience and, on a whim, called the office in Boston, and the Chief Medical Examiner was open to the idea of having an intern. That was a particularly busy office, and the morgue was so full that the bodies were lined up everywhere.

On my first day, I got a tour of the morgue and there he was, the first real "live" body, lying on a metal gurney in the hall between autopsy suites. Just lying there in jeans and a shirt, like nothing had happened. Other than the bullet hole in the side of his head, which had necessitated his trip to the morgue. I remember clearly, he was a white male with dark hair, perhaps in his mid-fifties, almost appearing to be asleep. When I walked by the body, I kept my eyes locked on the pale hand—waiting for it to move until I passed out of his reach.

The back doorbell rings, bringing me back to the present and my tasks. I go through the garage to see who is there. I peer at the video screen, note the uniform, and let the officer in.

He is a stocky man with a buzz cut to his dark hair. His metal nametag says "S. Hammond." He says, "I'm here for the possible suicide."

"Come on back." I lead him to where I'd left Dr. Ivanovic working his way through the various examination procedures necessary to determine manner and cause of death.

"What's the story?" I have to shout over the noise of the saw at the next table as cutting into a skull begins.

"He was found lying on the couch on the back porch of his house." The detective looks past me, as if he is confused about talking to me, looking around perhaps for a male investigator to speak with since many of the cops over forty I have met are still a part of the good-old-boys club and don't expect to have to talk to women in this context.

I started seven months ago as the first female Medicolegal Death Investigator, and the second to hold that position, in the history of the state's Northern District office. The Chief Medical Examiner's office in Richmond created the position a few years ago to help modernize the office, but the investigators haven't gained the respect or power to do the job effectively all the time. The position of Medicolegal Death Investigator is only two years old, so the police are still getting used to talking to us at all. Before us they would either talk to the doctor directly or just fax in their reports to the office and not even bother to come in.

"He was a drunk and a loner, no there was no doctor available or willing to sign," Hammond continues. I nod and scratch some quick notes in my logbook for this case. If a person is found outside or in an unsecured location, an autopsy is needed. This doubles the reason for the body being here. The types of deaths that are considered Medical Examiner's cases are homicides, suicides, accidents or deaths with no doctor to sign the death certificate, and any other suspicious deaths. Now, I tell people to go to the doctor so they will have someone who is aware of their medical history and could sign off on their death certificate to avoid getting an autopsy.

"It should be straightforward, then." I look directly into Hammond's hazel eyes and smile sweetly to disarm him. I still am not sure how to act; I feel like I have to be partly authoritarian, partly feminine, but still competent and myself.

I leave Officer Hammond and Dr. Ivanovic and make my rounds of the doctors and tables, asking each if they are in need of help, taking pictures or reading notes at the different stations and generally trying to be useful and provide information when necessary.

One of the other pathologists is my direct boss, Catherine Reeves, a brilliant woman, who is passionate about her work. Today she is working on a death from an accident. She graduated from Harvard Medical School and takes her role as final caregiver seriously. With the back of her bent wrist, she pushes her light-brown hair from her striking gray eyes that are framed by safety glasses.

"Hey Julia, can you come here?" She looks up at me for the first time today. There are no police officers near her, as I have noticed that many of them don't know how to handle her intensity and intelligence; they are a bit awed and perhaps even frightened. She has a thirst for knowledge but is sometimes halted by others' lack of understanding.

I walk to her side and look at the body on the table in front of her. He's a white-haired man who looks to be in his seventies. The skin of his chest cavity is pulled open, and Matt, the diener, is leaning in to use hedge clippers to cut out the sternum to open up the rib cage. The sternum or breastbone is where the ribs attach in the middle of our bodies and needs to be removed in order to examine the organs. Dr. Reeves reaches in with a scalpel and sighs as she pulls out his heart. "I'm looking for evidence of an electrocution. Sometimes you can see signs of it in the heart." She places down the red, slimy organ, about the size of a grapefruit, and walks to the corpse's bare feet. She points at his white toes, and I see a black mark that looks like a burn on the bottom of his right foot.

"This is an indicator of an electrocution. He was trimming trees on a metal ladder and hit an electrical line with his clipper. The electricity has to find a way to the ground, and he was the route it took."

I bend down to examine the dark stain. It looks like he had put out a cigarette on the bottom of his foot. "Wow, fascinating."

I learned about this phenomenon in the pathology class I took during my graduate training at George Washington University, but had not seen it in person until now. Dr. Reeves often has a fascinating tidbit to share and I enjoy hearing her thoughts.

I lean closer and say, "Interesting," looking back at the organs but not seeing what she could see in the dark-red mass of his heart.

"Hey guys." Our lead investigator's loud voice suddenly reverberates through the room, causing most people to look his way. Patrick really likes to make an entrance. He strides through the double doors and heads for the law enforcement officers still huddling in their protective circle. In the police department he came from, there was a mandatory retirement policy at twenty years, so many officers like Patrick retired in their mid forties and had a whole other career afterward. Not a bad gig.

For many of the years that he was on "the force," Patrick was the favorite detective of the acting Chief Medical Examiner, Dr. Drew Deland. That certainly helped Patrick be a shoo-in for the job when it was created in 2000—just in time for his retirement from the police department. So it worked out perfectly for him.

A loud buzzing cracks through the room again. Matt had been in the back and now enters with a male detective I sort of recognize (a lot of them blend together) from Fauquier County. He has brought along a young female intern to what I assume is her first autopsy. She is a slim, attractive woman wearing her blonde hair in a ponytail. She smiles at me as we all make our way into the morgue. I smile back, knowing how she is feeling being the newbie.

I see Patrick push his muscular shoulders back and stand up straighter in an attempt to make his five feet seven seem bigger. Then he makes his way to the couple. Patrick is drawn to young, attractive women. When I first started the job, he tried to impress me, and even though I look young I have always felt older than my years. I know it bothers him that I'm not star struck with him or his accomplishments. At first I was polite and interested in his stories, but when it became clear to him that I saw him as another person, not an all-knowing deity, his affection for me lessened. I get the sense that he needs the oohing and ahhing that I just can't bring myself to do. Plus I know it drives him crazy that my shoes make me nearly his height. Definitely seems like some Napoleon complex there.

"Hey! How are you doing?" He extends his hand, leaning forward smiling, overplaying the connection to the newly entered detective. The three chat for a bit, then Patrick assumes his self-imposed role of alpha male of the office to take lead of the intern. The woman looks about twenty-one or so and very eager to please. She has on heavy blue eye shadow and mascara, perhaps to make her look older, but she is still cute. I roll my eyes when she gives him the desired look of adoration.

"Hey Drew." Patrick sidles up to the oldest pathologist in the office, Dr. Drew Deland, a short, balding man. The young woman is wide-eyed and eager to see the body of the suicide. Drew perks up when he sees the young woman behind Patrick.

Dr. Drew Deland has worked here for fifteen years. He survived many years of ridicule from the previous Chief Medical Examiner who, I was told, was an old-school dictator who yelled at everyone who entered the office. Dr. Deland, with his short, rotund body, now takes his position of authority to heart and definitely shows preferences. I am still learning everyone's personalities and the dynamics of the office. It is strange, almost like high school, but smaller.

The suicide, a white male, lies face up, naked on the metal table. His skin is off-white with undertones of yellow and blue, the skin sagging off of his body. Blotches of pink color and tufts of hair are scattered across his body. Dr. Deland points at the decedent's neck, where a pinkish-red, linear indentation runs from ear to ear, under the chin. "We already took off the rope," he says. "This mark is consistent with a suicide." He gestures to another steel gurney, where the man's clothing and a heavy, light-gray rope lie. I can see the knot on the noose, and that the rope was cut a few feet above the knot, rather than untied.

It is necessary to keep the knot intact for evidentiary reasons. If the type of knot is out of the skill set of the person who killed himself (according to witness accounts), it would be a clue that perhaps someone else tied it.

Patrick nods, crosses his arms, stands up straighter, and assumes his teacher stance. "The way the ligature crosses the neck is one way you can tell if a person hung himself." His eyes are dancing over the figure of the intern.

Patrick moves to a small metal rolling table and picks up some of the scene photographs included in the file. I walk over and look over his shoulder. In the image is the same man that is on the table but he is leaning forward, on his knees, held upright by a rope that is tied to a pull up bar in a doorway. His tongue protrudes from his mouth and is dark blue and red in color, and there is dried saliva and foam frozen in a drip on the side of his face. Only the whites of his eyes are visible, as his graying irises have rolled back into his head, and his eyelids are slightly open.

The carpet has a 1970s look, burnt-orange shag with stains and dark spots. Below him are two dark bottles, the size and shape of whiskey bottles, possibly Jack Daniel's. Alcohol always takes the edge off before killing oneself; however, it simply serves as a further depressant for an already despondent person. A crumpled sheet of paper lies at his feet.

Patrick looks over to the same piece of paper now in a plastic bag on the rolling table next to us. He picks it up. "I'm Sorry" is scribbled in black permanent marker. Not much of a note, but sometimes that's all that's left behind. It is a myth that most people who commit suicide leave a note. Statistics show that only thirty percent of people who kill themselves leave a note explaining why they did it. I feel bad for all the unanswered questions the other seventy percent left for their friends and families. But many of those in that group don't have too many people who would question their motives at all, making it all the more sad.

The Fauquier County police officer who had been hanging back now inches closer. "This is my guy." He nods toward the body on the table closest to him, the suicide. The detective looks in his late fifties, at least forty pounds overweight, with a strong western Virginia accent. His thin hair is pushed back and, like many of the descendants of the Scotch-Irish who settled in the mountains, he has a ruddy yet pale complexion. "Talked to his wife—well, ex-wife—almost," he snorts. "Isn't it always women?" The words come out of his mouth without a second thought. A lesson I was sure he learned when very young, and it makes me feel sad and angry.

He blushes a bit when he becomes aware of the two women around him. Men are still getting used to having women in law enforcement. I wonder if men know how hard it is to be a woman; we didn't choose our sex in this life any more than they did.

"Anyway, I talked to his neighbor, who said his wife left him three weeks ago for another man. The ex-husband had not been going to work much recently; he was a mechanic, and had hit the booze hard." His eyebrows rose. "Any sign of foul play?"

The Dr. Deland's white curls shake with his head. "Nothing unusual. No defense wounds, no sign of anything other than the obvious. Toxicology results will take a while, but for right now it looks like a suicide."

The detective shrugs. "She might not have hung him, but she may as well have." He turns and walks away, out of the office without saying good-bye, while the other officer and the intern move to another table.

I stand there frozen, stunned by the rudeness and vitriol of his comment. People confuse me, and I am always surprised when someone is just blatantly rude. I am still adapting to the work environment. My youthful experiences have not prepared me for the personalities and complexities of the "real world."

Even though I have been looking at dead people all day, I realize how hungry I am, so I change my shoes, grab my purse, and head out for some fast-food tacos from a place around the corner. I eat in my car just to be able to have silence since, as a true introvert, being around people saps my energy.

After lunch I head back to my office to work on writing reports and gathering information—and walk into Patrick yelling into the phone. "I can't talk to you right now, dammit!"

He turns and glances up, jumping as he notices me, and then looks away. Anger emanates from his body. His normally pleasant face is flushed and his mustache highlights the grimace on his lips. I feel the anxious energy radiating from him and want to get away from it as soon as possible. I am typing at my desk when Patrick stomps over and gives me a look. I stop and glance up at him. "Yes?"

"Can you take call for me tonight? Something's come up. I'll take call over this weekend then." Patrick's face darkens as he glances away.

"On call" here means that if there is a death report to take, we could be called to either let us know that a body is coming in or get permission to have a local ME do the external exam, on the rare occasion we would be called out to a scene. We each take call for a week and switch off the Monday morning of the week. I have taken numerous death calls at home but have only been called out to three scenes from home. It is Thursday, and one more day of being on call won't make much of a difference to my social life. The bonus aspect is that Patrick will take a day for me later when I want to switch.

"Sure, no problem." I don't want to pry; dealing with my own life is enough for me to think about, never mind someone else's issues.

"Thanks. I got to leave early." He walks over to his desk, shuts down his computer, and leaves the office.

A few minutes after he leaves the tension in the room deflates, and I am glad to be alone. My mind drifts back to my facial reconstruction, and I pull out Dr. Cuezze's e-mail and send him a quick note to thank him for his help. Then I quickly do an Internet search for his name. In a few seconds he is staring at me, a handsome face with dark, piercing eyes. I smile and flush.

In my thank-you e-mail I had attached a picture that Brian had taken of me working on the skull. It is a picture I like, with my black hair falling around my face while I am looking into the eyes of the sculpture. Maybe that will get Dr. Cuezze to respond sooner. I smile and sigh.

The rest of the afternoon is quiet and routine; I work until my usual time of 4:00, go home to my cats, and have a quiet night in.

CHAPTER 3

That night I find myself awake with the cold, cordless house phone against my ear.

"Hello?" I glance at the clock's glowing red numbers—12:23 a.m.—and try to focus on the voice on the other end of the line. Each of my two cats is tucked on either side of me, keeping me in place. I hear the voice of my friend Lisa Byrd on the phone. "Hey Jules, got a traffic accident here. I know, I know, you normally don't take traffics on call, but this one is weird and I'd appreciate your help."

Normally the annoying beep of my pager would go off for a death call, but since Lisa knows my home number and we are friends, she uses it to dial me directly. But this is no friendly call; I can tell she is in business mode.

I rub my eyes and sit up. "What's up?" I croak. I had answered the phone before actually waking up and am just realizing what is happening. I have only been asleep two hours and was in the deepest part of unconsciousness.

"White male, fifty-three years of age, single-vehicle accident. The car was reported off the road by a passer-by, and we found the body in the vehicle."

"So what's the weird part?" My brain is foggy and I am not connecting the dots.

"His watch face is broken, but there is nothing visible for it to have hit against. There is some other weirdness, too, but I want your opinion on it. Oh yeah, drug paraphernalia was also found in the car. The EMS have come and gone. I just think the body should come in for a full autopsy."

Deaths that occur by seemingly obvious means, including car accidents, can be taken to the closest hospital, where the body is examined by on-call medical examiners. An on-call ME is a person who is a doctor, but usually not a pathologist, and most definitely not a forensic pathologist. The doctors who sign up for being an on-call medical examiner do it for the excitement of it, or just the extra $50 fee per death certificate signed. They are not authorized to perform full autopsies, just external examinations and taking the blood for toxicology.

I trust Lisa's opinion so I am already convinced, but hearing about the drugs clinches it. "Okay. Take lots of pictures. Give me the location, and I'll be there as soon as possible. See you soon." I say.

"Thanks." She replies before hanging up.

With drugs present a full analysis must be done, as the deal then becomes suspicious or questionable. Did the drugs cause the accident? Or could it be considered an overdose? There are so many possibilities.

I switch on the bedside lamp and flinch at the bright light. I grab a pen from the mug I use as a pen cup that rests on the nightstand. I scribble the address and date and time then continue to fill out the "First Call" sheet that is on a pad I keep on the bedside stand. I drag my legs from under the warm comforter to start moving. It is my responsibility to go to the scene and retrieve the body. For a few seconds I sit motionless on the edge of the mattress, still waking up, then finally pull myself off the bed.

When going to a call-out, office policy requires us to respond in less than an hour from when the call is received. This is out of respect for the people at the scene and the public. The police have to keep the scene closed, and in this case it will also slow down traffic. There is much to do, and I have to stay focused. I still have to get dressed, drive to the office, pick up my scene kit, and go to the location in the transportation van. Unlike in some police work, we do not take work vehicles home.

The death investigators can serve as the transport service for the body when we go to a death call. If it is something that we cannot handle, then we have the option to call a funeral home, but that costs the office money and takes more time, waiting for them to show up.

I make it out of my apartment quickly and enter into the dark and clear night. There is a still crispness in the air and a sweet smell of the flowers growing in the apartment complex. In less than thirty minutes, I am in the white Medical Examiner's Office van pulling out onto Braddock Road. The darkness is broken by streaks of headlights passing by on the back roads. The van is still cold, and I shiver in my seat waiting for the heater to start working. I am glad I still have some of my long underwear from growing up near Saratoga Springs in upstate New York, but I am still a wuss about the cold.

After several miles of meandering up Route 123, I continue driving west on Route 50. I am hoping there will be no accident to slow me down, and then realize that an accident is exactly where I am going.

The Virginia medical examiner system is a statewide organization with four offices. The offices started with the Central Office in the state capital, Richmond, then Norfolk, Roanoke, and finally in Fairfax. My office covers fourteen counties in the northern and western parts of Virginia all the way to the West Virginia border, and includes a population of over two million. That means that all deaths requiring autopsies have to be brought to the Central Office. Northern Virginia is the most populated area in the state, holding approximately three million of the state's eight million total.

Classical music from the radio keeps me company as I drive toward where I have a vague idea the accident is located. The streets become less populated with fewer buildings as I drive away from town, and darkness fills the canvas of the windshield.

The scene becomes easy to locate when the red and blue flashing lights come into view. It is late at night, in my mind, and I think any sane person should be in bed, but there is still a good bit of traffic buildup, as the highway patrol has closed one of the two lanes to preserve the scene.

As I get close to it, my palms start to sweat and my heart beats faster. Going to a scene gives me a nervous thrill. To be part of the machine, not a watcher, but someone allowed into the restricted area. Even though my vehicle has no lights on it, I easily make my way around the other cars.

A police officer in a puffy jacket and hat guards the perimeter with his hand up. I pull up alongside him and show him my "Medicolegal Death Investigator" badge. I don't recognize him, but his face changes from annoyance to relief when he reads my credentials. I know they must have been out here for at least an hour, so I'm sure he is ready to leave the scene and get back into his warm car. He nods and waves me through. I peer over the three other police cars parked haphazardly on the side of the road, looking to find a place to park that is close enough to the scene but still out of the way of everyone else. Not an easy thing to do. In the van I sit high up, and it is helpful to be able to see over most cars. I suddenly realize why people are buying huge SUVs and trucks.

I step out of the van and shiver, the weather seeming colder after I have gotten used to the warm vehicle. I pull out my bag with my investigation gear. This includes notepads, evidence release forms, a camera, extra batteries and memory cards for the camera, several pairs of latex gloves, business cards, and pens. I try to keep the bag fully stocked, as it is a terrible feeling to enter a scene and not be prepared. I approach the group of officers standing next to the vehicles, who have light flashing off the metal on their hats, badges, and various shiny pieces on their uniforms. An older male officer I've met before smiles at me. "Officer Byrd is down there with the vehicle." He nods toward the ravine that borders the dark

Virginia woods. I look past the edge of the road and see the tail end of a vehicle and an oasis of lights from a portable light source about fifteen feet down the hill.

As I approach the vehicle, I see Lisa leaning over it. She is half Swedish-American and half Scottish, with a beautiful mane of blonde hair she keeps in a bun at work. At five foot ten, she towers over me—an advantage over other women in the force, but she has still has to fight for equal treatment the way all females in law enforcement have to. None of the four other male officers there are helping her.

She is wearing her Virginia State Police uniform with the hat at a forward tilt, her hair tucked up under it. The uniform is a bland tan, almost gray, color with a large Virginia State Police patch in gold on the shoulders. Plus a thin black tie, nametag, and belt full of police gear that I know weighs over twenty pounds.

She smiles at me. "Hey girl. Thanks for coming out."

"Hey girl." I say.

The vehicle sitting in the moist grass is a beat-up, light-blue Toyota Camry that looks like it was made in the late 1980s. It is nose down in a ditch with the front crumpled and the tail elevated about a foot into the air. Even with the shadows, I can see that the interior is showing its age. The light-colored rug is stained in patterns that looked like liquid spills, faded in various places with litter and fast-food wrappers crumpled and scattered throughout. In the driver's seat a white man, appearing to be somewhere in a rough middle age, is slumped forward onto the steering wheel.

The grass crunches under my feet as I move forward. I thank myself for wearing the right footwear—heavy work boots that enable me to easily walk on various terrains without falling—so I make it intact to Lisa's side next to the open passenger door.

"His wallet was in the glove compartment." She hands me the man's driver's license, already in a clear plastic bag. It is a faded piece of worn plastic, expired two years ago, the face staring out pale and drawn, his hair still mostly a dark brown. At least ten years younger than the man lying in front of me, his gray eyes staring out under heavy lids. I read a hard lifestyle on his face. The name on the license states, "Robert Greeley" and shows his date of birth as February 11, 1954, and an address in Manassas Park, about twenty miles southeast of where we stand. I ready my clipboard and pen to take notes.

I slowly move to the driver's side, taking my time navigating over the dark ground. It is difficult to do without touching the car for support. I am not sure if they are going to dust the car for prints and don't want to smudge any potential evidence.

As I look down all I see is the blackness of my feet disappearing into the grass, so it takes me a few minutes to get to the driver's door. I pull on the latex gloves that I keep in my pocket and open the door, making sure not to slide my fingers on the handle in case there are any fingerprints to be found.

Even though at first glance this looks like a traffic accident, I have been trained to treat every death as a homicide, to take care of every movement so as not to disturb any possible evidence, and to document all aspects of the scene step by step. We get only one chance to document the crime scene; after that everything is altered by subsequent examinations. This makes anything we find potentially less convincing as evidence if the case ever goes to trial.

There is a triad system to documenting a crime scene. Note taking, photographs, and diagrams. These help any investigator remember the scene when writing the report and perhaps later, testifying in court. Sometimes it can take years to go to trial on a case. Sometimes a case will go to appeal over and over, for not just years but decades. So it would be impossible to remember every detail of a scene. Even as memorable as a person might think an event is at that moment, those memories do fade after time—thankfully. I have to admit that already in my own short career, the memories of scene after scene are starting to bleed together.

I snap pictures with the digital camera hanging around my neck. I take a few overall shots of the scene knowing I can rely on Lisa's crime scene photos for more photographs, as police crime scene investigators take dozens if not hundreds of them. I don't trust all the investigators I have worked with, but I know that Lisa is thorough, but also human. I also know she is responsive and gives us copies of her digital photographs right away, unlike some of the other jurisdictions we work with.

I peer through the glass of the window that is cracked open two inches and foggy from grime and smoke.

After taking a few initial photographs to show the status of the door before I touch it, I pull it open slowly. As the door opens, his body shifts and starts sagging toward the passenger side—but doesn't quite fall over. I hold my breath then inhale in a gasp when I know he isn't moving toward me. I feel I have to act tough, efficient, and professional and repress the squeamishness that is perfectly natural to any sane person.

The dead man is wearing a thin, tan windbreaker with, "Members Only" written on the left breast pocket, with scraggly, salt-and-pepper hair strands swirling around the back of his neck.

The flesh on his the face that previously held any expression is now melted forward where gravity took it. There is a deep gash on the front of his head, and his hair is short enough to show the dark-red stains on his forehead and tracks of dried blood trailing down the front and sides of his slack, squashed, and wrinkled face. The skin under his eyes are dark and have what we call "raccoon eyes," which is often a result of intracranial bruising.

Being a child of the '70s, I spent my formative years watching horror movie after horror movie, most of them starring some sort of undead terror. The vision of Jason coming out of the lake at the end of the movie *Friday the 13th* has been emblazoned in my mind forever, and I am still convinced that there's a corpse in every body of water. This job does not help to fight that theory.

I shake my head and remind myself why I am here. It is my job to focus on finding clues on the body. To be the eyes and ears of the doctors who will examine the body at the morgue the next day. That is what makes this fulfilling to do. If I ever just stumbled upon a body, I know I would probably scream. I squeeze the camera to bring myself into the moment and make sure it does not touch anything at the scene.

The man is wearing a flannel shirt and jeans with a white T-shirt peeking out from under it. My gloved hand hovers above his face. "May I?" I glance up at Lisa for permission to touch him.

"We were waiting for you," she states.

"Thank you." I am just being polite; in Virginia, the Medical Examiner's Office has jurisdiction over any body that is found. The police are required by law to wait for permission from the ME's office to move the body. That permission can come over the phone or in person, so, lucky for me, it is not necessary for personnel from the ME's office to attend every death scene.

I slowly pull the man's head back with my right hand, noticing that it is a little heavy and stiff almost to the point of immobility. This means that rigor mortis has not set in fully. Rigor mortis is when the acids in the body settle into the muscles and make them harden in the position that the person was in when they died. Rigor usually starts after about four hours and is set fully at twelve hours. It abates somewhere between twenty-four and thirty-six hours and doesn't come back. These are not hard-and-fast rules but a general outline that has been found by research into determining the time of death or postmortem interval.

"Who called this in?" I ask Lisa over the car hood.

"Someone driving by who saw taillights in the ravine about two hours ago."

That makes sense. Two hours might seem like a long time, but considering how long it takes for the police to respond, set up the area, and then the time it took me to get there, two hours seems reasonable.

Under the splattering of blood on the man's face, I see the reddening color of pooling blood beneath the skin. The man's nose is distorted, pushed to the side. The lividity pattern seems inconsistent with his position. There is a random blotchy pattern across his skin that also doesn't make sense.

It might be from the impact with the steering wheel. But the distortion is not consistent with hitting a round object. It seems flatter in shape than what I expect from just the force of hitting the wheel. His body also seems to be pulled too far forward. I know some people don't mind being that close to the wheel when they drive, but here it looks abnormal. "This guy is a bit close to the wheel, don't you think?"

"I was waiting to see if you noticed that, too."

I lean in toward the corpse and shine the light onto his eyes. Being this close to a dead face always freaks me out. I have to banish all the flashbacks from the horror movies where the supposedly dead guy's eyes suddenly widen and the corpse comes to life. I grip his jaw with my gloved hands and try to move it back and forth to determine the level of rigor mortis. It doesn't move at all— rigor starts in the smaller muscles then moves to the larger parts of the body.

"Yeah, this is definitely questionable, good call." I raise my voice to Lisa, knowing there are other officers nearby who have been commenting on the futility of waiting for me and on her suspicions that this was more than an accident.

I lift the man's right wrist, where there is a round-faced watch with a leather band. The face is shattered with a spiderlike pattern of cracks through the glass.

I take photographs of the watch, and the rest of the scene, then measurements of the scene. "Are you going to process the car?" I call to Lisa.

"Yeah, the tow truck is here and is taking it to the garage. Rick is going to meet me."

I nod pleased, knowing that Lisa will do a thorough job with the car and the evidence in it. The current location is too precarious to examine the car efficiently. I recall seeing the tow truck waiting when I pulled up to the scene, and I know the driver will be eager to get going. There is a garage at the police station, where they will take the vehicle to do a thorough examination. After a few more notes and photos, it's time to move the body.

"Let's just get the body out when the car is pulled out of the ravine." I say. "It would be too hard to bring him up this hill."

"Good idea." Lisa says and bends her head into the radio to tell an officer to let the tow truck driver know we're ready to move the car. Soon we hear the shrill beeping of the tow truck reversing and the sound pierces through the dark night.

The crank is luckily long enough and two of the policemen who were on top of the hill come down with the tow truck driver. The driver is bear like, with a bushy beard and sturdy body. He steadies his way down while pulling the heavy chain and hook down to the car.

Within thirty minutes the car is up on solid ground. Now it will be much easier to get the dead body from the car into my van.

The shadows of all the spotlights are moving around me as I go to the back of the van. There are two gurneys secured to the vehicle. I reach in and pull, the metal liter sliding out of the van easily. Once half of the gurney is out I pull the wheeled legs down and the other side pops out easily. The large, black wheels make it possible to roll over the rock and dirt on the side of the road. Lisa comes over to assist and we move it as close as we can to the car.

I pull open the black, nylon body bag that was on the gurney and spread it out flat, and pull the zipper open with a buzz. I open a clean, white sheet that is prepackaged inside the body bag in a clear plastic bag, for catching any trace evidence from the body. Once that is opened and laid out the maneuvering of the body begins.

It is hard enough to carry a full sized human being when they are alive, but so much more difficult when the person is no longer helping at all. We work his legs out, check to make sure he is not caught on anything and manage to move the body onto the gurney before the body goes into full rigor. Full rigor mortis makes it that much more difficult to position a person on a gurney in a way that they can be strapped down. We load the body into my van, and it is now up to me to get it back to the morgue. Sometimes an officer will escort me, but not tonight as it is late and everyone wants to get home. I know that Lisa will be back in the morning to take photos at the autopsy. I want to let her get to her own business and hopefully eat something before she comes to the Medical Examiner's office the next day (or today, really). She won't be getting any sleep before then.

As I drive away, I see in my rearview mirror the officers begin to take down the markers and orange cones to release the scene.

CHAPTER 4

I manage to get back to the office and check the body into the cooler just as the sky begins to lighten. I run home to steal a few hours of sleep before returning to the office. After the adrenaline rush wears off, exhaustion creeps over me and I am able to fall asleep around 3:30, fully dressed on top of the bedcovers. I return to work at 8:00 a.m., this time wearing flat shoes, a pullover shirt, and some wash-and-wear pants, with my hair twisted up in a clip and no makeup; a sure sign that I am not feeling perky. Now the real work starts, printing my photographs and writing up a report for the pathologists to review.

When I make it to the morgue, I find Lisa already there taking photographs. She is standing on a set of metal stairs that can be rolled to the desired position to take ninety-degree-angle photographs of the body from above. Her hair is back in a ponytail now, and she has changed into tactical pants and a polo shirt. These clothes are much easier to move around in than the regular uniform. She is training to perform forensic work at her job and has a hard time splitting her focus between that and regular patrol duty, especially when the sergeant on duty isn't feeling generous.

Detective Rick Sentor is also present, a twenty-year veteran of the Virginia State Police, and a detective who has been doing crime scene investigation for fifteen of those years. He has been a mentor for Lisa and also teaches me a lot when he comes to the morgue. Much has changed and advanced in that time, but he is a rare old-timer who is actually excited about learning new techniques as well as training the next generation to do the job well in the future.

For safety Rick is holding the steps Lisa is perched on, even though they have rubber feet and a locking mechanism. Who says that chivalry is dead?

"Hey Rick, good morning" I greet him as I walk over to join them. He grins broadly, a nice paternal smile, not a creepy perverted one like I usually receive, and then he gives me a quick one-armed hug. He is one of the few people I work with whom I don't mind hugging at work.

"Hey, how you doin'? Sorry I missed you at the scene, I was at another car accident. Non-fatal so no clients for you." He chuckles and turns toward the body on the table, his hand still on the railing of the stairs.

"Good, glad I got some sleep. I bet Lisa didn't get any." I look at her adjusting her camera and seeming to be in a daze.

"Nope, not at all," Rick agrees.

Doug the diener is whistling away while preparing the tools and sink for the job at hand. His thick arms are muscular and covered in blond fuzz. A few weeks ago, I tried to handle the Stryker saw he uses and found it too daunting. The strength it takes to cut through the skull in a professional manner, not to mention move bodies around like rag dolls, is amazing.

"Hey Doug." I wave at him.

"Hey girl!" His voice resonates through the room. "Bringing me more bodies."

"Sorry Doug." I say back through a yawn.

He chuckles and starts whistling again, the tune clearly "Stairway to Heaven."

Doug is a Virginia native who has been working here for over fifteen years and seems to enjoy the work. He is pleasant to be around, somebody who likes routine and to keep his workstation clean, so he is an excellent fit for the job. He has a strong stomach and a macabre sense of humor, too, which are mandatory for the position.

"It looks like a homicide," I answer. "Found in a car on the side of Route 50. Who is the doctor handling the case?"

Doug gets in at 6:00 a.m. and spends the morning up front with the office managers and knows what's is going on.

"I think its Dr. Reeves day today. It was supposed to be Dr. Deland, but he got called into court this morning." He snorts his displeasure; he is not Dr. Reeves's biggest fan, as she takes longer than the other doctors to do a thorough autopsy. Dr. Deland works the most quickly, doing an autopsy in less than an hour, where Dr. Reeves might take over two hours, as she is thorough and wants to analyze all aspects of the patient. "Oh yeah, and Patrick is out sick today."

"No problem. I hope he isn't too sick." I hadn't noticed that his area was empty when I got in. I am still in a fog from lack of sleep. I am definitely one of those people who functions best on seven hours of sleep. "How many bodies do we have today?"

"Just the one you brought last night. Nothing left over from yesterday, so that's good."

With only a few bodies in the office, it's not a big deal that Patrick is off. He isn't missing anything, since the only cops in today are Lisa and Rick; neither of them is enamored of him, anyway.

"This is a pretty interesting situation," Rick says. "I was out at another location so couldn't come to the scene last night. But back at the garage, we found some strange stuff in the trunk. Some soil, and some other items, but the soil was compacted, in shapes, like from some sort of tread, shoe or tire, not sure yet. If it's tire, then the shape isn't from any car tire I've ever seen. Lisa's got some photos she can show you when she gets down."

Lisa rattles down the metal stairs, pulls the camera strap from around her neck, and places the camera on the table in the corner. Then she stands up straight and rubs her neck from the strain of the camera weight. Rick watches his protégée at work and seems pleased with her thoroughness.

Doug is now stripping the body of its clothing, not an easy task without the usual live-person cooperation. Arms and legs become obstacles to just get fabric over. No lifting of the butt to pull off the pants that, too, has to be done manually. When the body is ready, Lisa rattles back up the stairs with the camera. The next set of photographs will be taken with the body nude, to show any evidence of injury to its exterior.

When she's done Lisa climbs down and walks over to the table in the corner and takes a swig of coffee from a lidded paper cup. The old table is now used as a clean place for police officers to set up their equipment. As a general rule, no biohazards are placed on it. Just drugs. We are required to document all the medications that we bring in with a body. These medications help the doctors figure the contributing factors to death. Whenever medication comes in, we compare each of the pills and the numbers stamped on them to the *Physicians' Desk Reference* or *PDR* to verify what the medication is and for what condition it's generally prescribed. The *PDR* is an enormous book, inches thick and probably at least five pounds in weight. It can sometimes take hours to look through when there are multiple medications, as we have to find the individual section, which has a picture of the pill to scale and all the information about it.

After we verify the pills, we count them to learn if the patient has taken the prescribed amount or more, which can contribute to the cause of death, and to make sure none are taken from the office. More CYA—or cover your ass. I have read about a Medical Examiner's office somewhere in the South where medication was going missing and being sold illegally by the staff. I had no idea that one pill of OxyContin can go for $10 a pill.

I hope that we are getting all the details necessary. This contrasts with my body's screaming desire to go back to sleep. I am sure Lisa's body is worse. But it is protocol and pride for a person who starts a scene to work it through to its conclusion.

Lisa looks tired and gaunt, with her blue eyes sunken into her skull. She has a halo of golden flyaway strands around her face that escaped from her ponytail, but she looks happy and satisfied.

"Pretty curious." She is sipping coffee through the hole in the lid and swaying like a hummingbird drinks from a flower. She is jittery, almost vibrating.

"How many cups have you had?" I ask, smiling.

"Enough to keep me awake and alert. So . . . maybe six."

"I hope you can get to sleep in a few hours!"

"No worries. With my blackout curtains, white-noise machine, and this exhaustion, I'll be out for ten hours. But look what we found."

She gets the camera and turns it on to scroll through the photographs stored on it. She finds the image she wants and turns the screen toward me. I take the camera and peer into the screen.

It shows tiny, rectangular squares of compacted dirt, adjacent to cross-shaped pieces of dirt. Next to the small paper-scale crime scene added to the picture, I see that the dirt shapes are no larger than five centimeters. I recognize the shapes.

"These look like mountain bike tire treads. My college roommate was into biking. You could probably check local shops to match tires; I don't know if there's a database for bicycle tire tread. I think I have more pictures of this." I pull out the photos that I printed out earlier and find one that shows the Toyota's trunk. "There—you can see them in this picture, too." The dirt is also seen from a different angle than Lisa's picture. "Great, can I get a copy of yours, too? I want to do some research."

She nods. "I knew it wasn't from a car . . . I positively need to look into it."

Doug calls Lisa over, indicating that the body is ready for the next set of photographs. Robert Greeley is now lying face down. Lisa again climbs the five steps to nowhere and again begins taking photographs.

I walk over to the table and look down at the decedent. His body has dried abrasions and bruises on his neck and head and down his shoulders. The pattern of abrasions is unusual. It is certainly not common in automotive accidents. The fact there are older bruises on his face is interesting, too, as the body only bruises when it is alive.

Dr. Reeves enters the morgue suite quietly. "Good morning." She is already suited up in a blue paper smock, a blue hat that looks like a shower cap, and blue paper booties over her shoes. She looks surprised to see so many people in the morgue for just one body.

We give her various noises of greetings. I hear Doug sigh behind me. "Here we go," he mutters.

The dance of the autopsy begins. Dr. Reeves's leans over the naked body, examining it inch by inch; first she looks at him as he was found, with all the dirt and the goo, then they use a sponge to wipe off the blood, fluids, and dirt that hide any real damage. Notations of every aspect of the examination are marked on the body diagram.

I walk up to Dr. Reeves and show her the printouts of my photographs of the body at the scene. She examines a particular five-by-seven print. "Hmm, the lividity looks different in this photograph. It doesn't match the position."

I nod. "That's what I thought, too, but I wanted your opinion."

With her gloved hands, she starts feeling his face and head. "Is the X-ray done?" she calls out to Doug. It is standard procedures to take X-rays of all bodies that come in for autopsy. That is supposed to be the first thing the technicians do in the morning before the autopsy is started. "I want to see the head X-ray," she says.

"The body images are on the table, but the head shot is developing now. You want me to go get it?" Doug is in full gear and raises his bloody hands—he clearly doesn't want to move.

"I'll get it," I say. The X-ray machine and developer are in the next room through another set of unobtrusive gray double doors. I go into the back and pull the X-ray from its metal developing case. I hold up the ridged, black sheet and see the outlines of the body but can't understand too much from the ghostlike shapes. I return to the main autopsy suite and hand Dr. Reeves the large X-ray film.

She removes her gloves and thrusts the film into place on the light box affixed to the wall. The lights in the box flicker then come to life and illuminate the faint white and gray forms imprinted into the film.

She points to the back part of the skull at a thin line that is barely visible to me. "This shows a hairline fracture radiating from deep on the bottom surface of the skull. This seems inconsistent with a car accident, and may in fact be a true basilar skull fracture. This is more common from a blow to the back of the head."

She shaves the decedent's head to get a better view of the skin under the hair. A doctor can determine if a person was alive after a trauma, since the body starts to heal right away. If there is no evidence of exsanguination, or bleeding, then it is apparent that the person's heart was not beating at the time of the trauma.

Dr. Reeves gingerly shaves around the back of the head, not using lubricant as there is no concern with razor burn, and reveals a dark area of skin under the hairline. The hair at that portion of the corpse's head is still more pepper than salt, and the marks would have been difficult to see through that area of his hair. Dr. Reeves nods. "Yes, this is definitely from a blow."

I am determined to take all the photographs she will need to help determine what happened. I always feel afraid that I will miss something, or not get the photograph in focus or otherwise make a mistake.

After I photograph the damage, she decides to go forward with examining his head before doing the body. Lisa snaps her own shots. Dr. Reeves makes a single slice from ear to ear, over the top of the head. Doug peels the skin away from the skull, using the scalpel to cut away the skin fibers that hold the scalp to the skull. They look like the thin strands of cotton candy that stick to the sides of the spinner in a cotton candy machine.

Damage to the forehead is kept to a minimum in case the funeral home has to put him back together in case the family wants to see him, or for an open-casket viewing.

The image is a gruesome one, though somehow I have gotten used to it. The flap of his scalp is folded down with the hair side covering the eyes and half the face. Doug approaches with the bone saw. This is basically a hand drill with a circular saw at the end of it, designed to cut through bone via vibration. He first cuts a notch in the front of the skull so that when it is placed back on the base, it will not slip off; and then he continues to cut circumferentially around the rest of the skull.

Once the top of the skull is removed, the brain is exposed sitting in its case, slimy and gelatinous. Gray, pink, and white, covered by a thin sheet of "dura mater" that keeps it in place. This is a thin, partially translucent, fibrous material through which the brain gets its blood, fluids, and nutrients. I am amazed at how mechanical our bodies are when broken down into pieces.

Doug uses pliers to pull the thin film, which reminds me of plastic wrap, away from the skull with a terrible ripping sound. This allows the doctor to examine the skull closely for intracranial hemorrhaging. If any bleeding comes from inside the dura mater, that indicates a cause inside the brain, like a stroke, whereas if blood is on outside the dura mater, that indicates a cause from something external, like a blow to the head.

Dr. Reeves is nodding to herself and scribbling notes onto her diagram, trying to record all her observations for later use when making her report. I take several photographs of each part of the skull that she points to. Doug measures each artifact and calls out the numbers that correlate to the drawing of the injury she's sketching. She nods.

"This definitely looks like a homicide. There's no way this damage to the back of the head would have come from the car accident. And even though his face is a little distorted from being against the steering wheel, its not as much as expected, and the lividity does not indicate he was in that forward position immediately after he died."

She pulls out the brain and lays it on the white plastic cutting board. She points to the front of the brain, which is darker and many more red veins around it.

"This is countercoup, which is more evidence that he was hit on the back of his head."

I peer closer and can see how the area of the brain near his eyes does look bruised. "Wow."

"It's when the front of the brain hits against the skull case and causes bruising." She points at the back of the skull. "Here there is also bruising, but less."

I look up to see Lisa and Rick next to me. Lisa is mesmerized. "So that means someone smashed him on the back of his head."

"I will put it all in my report," Dr. Reeves states.

The Y incision comes next, named for the shape that is cut into the chest cavity. The top two arms of the Y are positioned at the collarbones, with the bottom tip reaching down to the top of the pubic bone. Then the skin is peeled back from the body to examine the muscles for any subdural abrasions or other abnormalities. Depending on the size of the person, a layer of fat lies between the muscle and the skin, at least an inch, even on average-size people, and on heavy ones it is sometimes inches thick. It looks like a spongy yellow gel. Ever since I first saw this layer of fat up close, I've found it hard to overeat.

After the skin is opened, the muscles are pulled back, exposing the ribs. Then the ribs are cut with common branch clippers bought at the hardware store.

The sternum is cut out and the ribs pulled back like a flower blooming. This has also curbed my desire to eat short ribs and all sorts of BBQ.

The organs are then examined in the body, removed, weighed . . . brain: 1,200 grams, heart: 300 grams, liver, etc. The scale looks like what you find at the grocery to weigh your vegetables. Dr. Reeves carefully takes out each organ and examines it, calling out the weights. Then she dissects each piece, keeping parts for microscopic analysis.

Unbelievably, Lisa is still awake and makes it through the entire autopsy. When I can't help Dr. Reeves or Doug by taking pictures, moving items, or fetching documents for the doctor to review or to feed her information, I stand next to Lisa and Rick, arms crossed and legs shoulder-width apart, cop stance.

"So it does look like a homicide. Did you find out any more about this guy?"

Lisa nods and pulls out her notepad. "He was just out of prison three weeks ago. Living with his sister in a trailer park in Dumfries." Dumfries is a town in Prince William County about fifteen miles west of us.

"What was he in for?"

"Burglary, but it was his second time, so he was in for the last eight years. About nine years ago there was a rash of burglaries in those "McMansions" around the area, but we could only tie him to two. You remember that?"

I shake my head. I wasn't living in the area seven years ago. I was in the heart of the Catskill Mountains at the State University of New York at New Paltz finishing my bachelor's degree and in the midst of a romance.

I smile to myself at my fleeting memories of back then. Driving through the Catskill Mountains in upstate New York, cliff jumping and swimming in cool freshwater streams. How things have changed: heartbreak, several moves, graduate school, and now this. I never would have thought I would end up here outside the nation's capital.

Rick is still talking. "Yeah, there were several burglaries in McLean, Great Falls, and Alexandria. All took place in high-end homes, and only expensive items were stolen. There was a lot of press because even the assistants to politicians were hit." He chuckles. "You know how it is: It's all in who you know."

I nod. I am just starting to learn this lesson. Naively, I had believed that you could make it in life by doing a good job and hard work. But every year that goes by, I see more clearly how things are related. By friendships, family, sex, or money. I don't know if it is working in this field, getting older, or what, but I am definitely growing more cynical. Or maybe it's just how life is outside of confines of school.

It took me a long time to get a job in the field I wanted. My internship at the Boston Medical Examiner's office was pivotal, but it still took over a year. When I did get the position and was so excited—I may have overdone the effort by making a cake the first week I started. I really wanted everyone to be happy that I was there. After only six months of working here, I am learning how to balance being friendly with having a professional demeanor.

I enjoy learning anything and everything about the field of forensic science, meeting the doctors, police officers, and even attorneys. Plus, by being in the same building as the State of Virginia Division of Forensic Sciences, I get to meet the forensic scientists and explore all the forensic laboratory divisions I learned about during my master's degree studies.

"Anyway," Rick continues, "we had officers notify the next of kin this morning, and from what I heard they weren't too surprised. We'll look into what he's been up to. I'm going to combine all this information today and take a look at it, along with what I learn about his situation." He glances at Lisa, who is clearly dragging. "While she goes to sleep."

We head over to Dr. Reeves, who is standing at the cart starting to remove her gear. "So what do you think?" I ask her.

She still has the indentations on her pretty face from her mask and flyaway brown strands of hair around her face. "He was definitely moved." She is looking at the decedent. "Yeah, there was blunt-force trauma to the back of the head, the damage didn't match up with anything else in the car." She points to the diagram of the body.

Lisa is vibrating. "See? I told you it seemed funny to me." She bounces up and down on her toes.

"Let me know what else you find, but this will be ruled a homicide." Dr. Reeves removes her paper suit and walks out of the morgue.

"Good job," Rick says. "Now go get some sleep so you'll be of some use to me. Come back when you've gotten some rest."

CHAPTER 5

Well, Lisa certainly was right to have called me to the scene to look at the body. There seems to have been a staged homicide. But how? I don't remember there being any witnesses to the accident. But an ex-con has to have made some enemies. We will see.

After the autopsy is done, I stand next to the biohazard waste box near the exit and begin the regimen of taking off my personal protective equipment, or PPE. First the mask, then the paper shoes rustling like a potato chip bag, and last the gloves, depositing them in the large cardboard box lined with the red biohazard trash bag symbol. I take a deep breath as I step back into the main building, into "fresh" non-morgue air.

I feel like I am supposed to be friends with everyone in the office. Still learning to separate the two—it is work that brings everyone together, not a desire to be friends. I think this is hard for my personality, remnants of a people pleaser. I stop by the front desk, where I am always happy to see the office secretary, Mary Lou Jenning, and her smiling face. Mary Lou is a jolly woman with a pink face, round figure, and a friendly attitude. She has an easy laugh and a quick smile, perfect for welcoming the public. I admire that and sometimes wish I could be that way, too. Maybe one day.

Unlike me she did not seek to work with the dead. She was just glad to have a secure government job with health insurance and benefits to supplement her husband's income.

She won't go back into the morgue, where the dead people are, unless it is absolutely necessary. It rarely is, thanks to intercoms and phones. She handles the front desk, deals with funeral homes, the Office of Vital Records for death certificate issues, various law enforcement agencies, and sometimes the families of the decedents.

She has recently lost seventy pounds by cutting out pork rinds and midnight snacks and is reveling in her voluptuous new form. Her husband is a sanitation worker for the neighboring county to the west.

"How are you doing?" I ask, although in truth I feel too tired to listen to her answer. I am still learning how to fit in, get along, learn and do my job, and not get on anyone's bad side. I am not sure if I am succeeding. I am realizing that relationships and communication are the most important factors in how people in an office get along and operate smoothly together. The knowledge base is secondary, and can always be learned on the job.

After catching up on the activities of Mary Lou's husband and stepson, I get back to my office and find an e-mail reply from Dr. Cuezze already. Yay!

Julia,

It was a pleasure to speak with you last week. I am happy to help you in any way I can. I will be in DC next week for a meeting and was wondering if you would like to meet up. Let me know. ☺

Wow! I was hoping to meet him someday, but never thought it would be so soon. I type a reply: *Sounds like fun. Let me know when and where.*

Thoughts of the handsome Dr. Michael Cuezze put me on a giddy cloud. I think about relationships a lot and wonder if I will ever have a good partner or will be a good partner. I am only twenty-eight but have had my share of relationships and heartache.

I have always wanted to love and be loved, but the fear inside me has kept any man who got too close at arm's length. I'm still not ready to expose myself to anyone else. My memories of home are without a father at all, my mother at work, and mostly include my cat and grandmother as company. I was bullied in school, and it's hard for me to be vulnerable and to get close. But sometimes I feel so tender, and I cannot help it. Deep inside I still have hope and faith.

Every day someone from the Medical Examiner's Office has to take the blood removed from the bodies in the morgue to the Division of Forensic Science upstairs, where the toxicology laboratory analyzes it for drugs or alcohol. That information helps the doctors determine the cause and manner of death.

Today I will do the chore, because I want to see one of the two firearms examiners, Justice Levi Ferguson, someone I always enjoy seeing. I have a mentor-type relationship with him that developed after meeting him, when he came down to look at a gunshot wound on a body. I walk into the main office and grab the case filled with blood vials slated for toxicology analysis and yell out to the receptionist to let her know where I am headed.

I take the short flight of stairs one story up into the lobby of Forensic Science. Even though the Medical Examiner's Office is technically under the Virginia Department of Health, and Forensic Science is under the Department of Criminal Justice Services, they are always in the same building.

I am amazed at how young the field of forensic science really is. It was only in 1974 that the Division of Consolidated Laboratory Services, which includes the Bureau of Forensic Science, was created in Virginia. In 1990 the Bureau was reborn into a Division. I have heard rumors that they are now working to become a Department. I am not exactly sure what that means for them, but I am guessing it has something to do with funding, administration and authority.

The lobby is an open room much like a doctor's office, where the receptionist for the laboratory sits on the left side of the main doorway at a smaller window that looks into the administrative area. On the other side of the main door is a low receiving desk, where the two evidence technicians sit to receive and release evidence.

Once in a great while the waiting room is empty, but more often than not it is filled with police officers from all over the state. This laboratory analyzes evidence for all of northern Virginia and as far west to the border of West Virginia. The long drive makes many of the people who came to submit evidence pretty cranky.

Especially when there is heavy traffic followed by a long wait to submit evidence.

Last year the traffic in the D.C. area was ranked the third worst in the country, only slightly better or less bad than Los Angeles and New York City. When I moved down in 1998 from my rural upstate New York home, I was dismayed by the complexity of the D.C./Northern Virginia area map. Not just one sheet—a book. A book with many, many pages filled with roads, roads, and more roads.

Perched along these roads are businesses, houses, and townhouses—everywhere. Strip malls—everywhere. It was mind-boggling at first, but after about two years it seems normal to me. I don't know if that's good or bad.

In the lobby there are several police officers, each wearing a different colored uniform and shoulder patch indicating the various jurisdictions in the area. They grumble to one another about how long it is taking. There is a wait to submit evidence and an even longer wait to get it back. The backlog for drugs to be tested can extend up to six to eight months. Many court cases have been thrown out because of this delay, as the legal system required a speedy trial and the hold on the testing didn't allow for that to happen. These long wait times seem to be the result of too few analysts and too many cases coming in for processing.

The secretary is hiding from the mob behind her window with a high counter. I approach her and greet her.

"Good morning, Sabrina."

She looks at her watch. "Just past noon—so good afternoon." She smiles widely. She is a young, pretty African-American woman who always recognizes me and buzzes me in.

"Don't forget to sign in." She gestures to the sheet of paper on her desk. Most of the people in the lab know me by now, since I come up several times a week to submit blood samples for toxicology analysis. I still have to sign the log sheet for visitors, since technically I am one, and am going into the restricted back area where evidence is kept and analyzed. I am always let in easily and quickly, getting confused or evil glares from those waiting in the lobby.

Upon going through the doors, I walk the familiar-looking gray hallways that flow through the building. The decorator kept the style from both floors consistent. In this laboratory there are a DNA section, toxicology section, chemistry section, and firearms examination section.

The DNA section is the first area past the administrative area to my left and is signified only by a small plaque next to the door. This area is more secure than the others, as the chance of having a DNA sample contaminated is always a possibility, and everyone has DNA, and brings it in just by entering. Just like Locard said, evidence is always transferring. Anyone who enters has to give a buccal swab, or a swab from the cheek, for the elimination database. So unless you have a good reason to be there, you are not allowed.

Chemistry is the busiest section, as drugs are abundant and often found in relation with other activities like robberies and a host of property crimes. There is a window to look into the room, like a human zoo, where three white-coated analysts are measuring evidence and one is sitting in front of a computer at one of the desks. Thrilling.

My official destination is the toxicology unit, which sits toward the back of the building. This is a small unit consisting of only one analyst and an assistant; together they analyze all the blood samples from the morgue as well as other evidence brought in by police.

I enter the room and see a shorthaired woman wearing a laboratory coat standing at one of the tables holding a glass vial.

"More bodies?" Gina smiles and acts surprised. Gina is the assistant and always has a smile and a joke when I see her.

"Always. People don't stop dying." I smirk. "Not too many today, only one this morning." With delicate clinking I remove the vials from their holder, sign the evidence sheet, and have her sign, then take a copy of the chain of custody sheet. Chain of custody is a cornerstone of proper evidence handling. It shows where a piece of evidence is taken from, who handles it, analyzes it, and where it is stored, until it is taken to court. The chain is absolutely necessary, as many times in the past (and some in the present) a police officer or technician may have had questionable handling or storage methods for evidence. The chain of custody is a way to keep all of us organized, honest, and accountable.

Upon finishing up my formal business, I walk through the door to the back hallway, where I can pass the firearms and tool-mark section. I hope that Justice Levi will be near the door's window so he might see me and come out.

As I turn the corner, I see Justice Levi standing in the hallway, right in the doorway to his unit, looking in. Justice Levi has dark-chocolate skin and a build reminiscent of his football days. He still has the ability to be imposing and scary, or sweet like a teddy bear. Usually he chooses the second persona, at least with me.

"Hello, Julia, how are you?" His voice is welcoming.

"Hey Justice." I turn toward him. "I was just dropping off some toxicology."

"Come on in." He holds the door to the firearms unit open for me. I slide into the room, and emerge into what looks like a metal junkyard. The room is large and open but divided by tables, desks, and cabinets. Large steel tool cabinets sit full, some open and overflowing. There are four microscopes on the tables, two that have one scope, and two that are comparison microscopes, like the ones that I used in class.

A comparison microscope looks at two items at the same time to compare them, hence the name. I took a firearms examination course during graduate school and have basic theoretical knowledge but not too much hands-on experience, which, to me, is the fun part.

The senior firearms examiner, Jason Meeks, is perched on a chair at his computer, lost among the stuff. I smile and wave to him. "Hello."

"Hey! How are the bodies?" He smirks, and the white in his otherwise dark beard glistens.

"Oh, you know." I am still learning the small talk used in the forensic world. "No guns today, so less work for you."

"Good job." He gives me a thumbs-up and resumes his focus on the computer screen.

"Have you gotten the tour yet?" Justice Levi asks me.

"No, but I would love one." I can't believe I have been here this long but not had the time to explore the place. I like to think that I am mechanically inclined and enjoy playing with tools, so I am fascinated by all of the equipment and hardware and seeing all the different ways to manipulate metal. As an artist I have been using tools for many years and love to understand how things work.

Justice moves over to one of the large cabinets and pulls it open. It is full of handguns, sitting side by side, with a white label hanging off each firearm. "These are the comparison firearms. When we find fired cartridges, we use them to compare for markings, to see if it looks similar to a certain brand and caliber of gun. Or for parts when we find a firearm that doesn't work." He gestures around the room.

We push through the door to another room in the unit that I've never noticed before. There sits a large silver-colored tank with an opening facing us. "This is where we shoot the guns to obtain a comparison of the fired projectile," Justice says. We step next to the long box and I can see that it's a pretty deep tank, the open top revealing that it is about three-quarters full of water.

"We shoot into the tank and the water slows down the projectiles, or bullets. We can retrieve the bullets unharmed, since they're not going through any hard target."

He reaches over to a long pole with what looks like clay on the end. "This is how we recover the projectile when we shoot a gun for comparison to a suspect bullet. Hold on."

He steps out of the closed room and I stand there in the small room.

The door swings back open and he has headphones on, a gun in one hand, and in the other a second pair of orange headphones plus protective glasses. He hands them to me.

I put on the protective gear quickly, not sure what is coming next. Since Justice already is wearing his ear protection and his regular glasses, he is ready. I'm sure I look like a dork wearing the gear, but it is so important to use it.

He approaches the water tank, aims, and fires twice. The bang reverberates through the room and I involuntarily jump. I have fired guns in the past, but still am not super comfortable with them. I have an intense respect of their power and regularly see the damage they can do.

We fish out the projectiles with the pole, swirling it into the clear water and pulling them out with a net. I take them into my hand and examine them.

Justice says, "This is the actual bullet in my right hand, and in my left, that's just the projectile." He holds the small metal item in his palm. "People use the term *bullet* incorrectly all the time—it drives me nuts. An actual unspent cartridge is what people call a bullet, but the correct terms are *cartridge* for the cylindrical part, and the bullet is what is pushed out of the cartridge, which, depending on the type of firearm, will either stay in the gun, if it is a revolver, or be ejected if it is a semiautomatic or an automatic."

I nod, remembering this from my firearms class. The cartridges are a brass color, smooth on the cylinder sides, hollow on one end where the bullet and gunpowder (lead, antimony, and barium) go, and on the other a flat cover with a circle in the middle and "BHA" and "40 S&W" stamped into the metal.

"What does the BHA stand for?" I ask, as my knowledge of gun manufactures is limited.

"It is Black Hills Ammunition, out in the Dakotas. They started in the early 80s and are used a lot by law enforcement and military. The number, the 40, is the caliber of the cartridge." He explains.

"Let's take a look." We walk into the main room and sidle up to a comparison microscope. "You can tell a lot with this evidence." He secures one cartridge to each side of the comparison microscope's stages with a pliable wax that he rolled between his fingers. "We know for a fact that these came from the same gun, since we just shot it ourselves. If we look at them under a microscope, we can see the physical evidence of that." He rotates the dials of the microscope to get the images lined up. He steps back and gestures toward the scope. I move forward and peer into the eyepieces I can see the image of both cartridges with a line down the middle separating the two.

Justice Levi points to the microscope dials. "You can rotate it here to show more or less of either side."

I rotate the dials to focus so I can see the details clearly. On the screen I see the round shape of the cartridge and the silvery island in the middle of the cartridge. There is an indentation in each.

"Different firearms will either shoot center fire, or rim fire, meaning that the firing pin will hit the center or rim of the primer cap to ignite the powder charge contained in the cartridge and firing it from the gun. Each firearm has its own imprint that it leaves on the fired projectile. Maybe black, concentric circles, parallel lines, or other specific marks that we can match."

As I peer closer at the image, I see some of what he was describing and that the images from each side are very similar. He pulls out another cartridge and replaces one side with the new item. "Take a look now."

Having seen the cartridges fired from the same gun side by side, I can now see the differences stand out with this new cartridge. It has very different marks from the first. Wow, the variations seem so obvious when they are next to each other.

"Now, we can't always match exactly, as the firearm does wear so the marks do change slightly every time it's fired. And will change more with wear or rust. Sometimes it's a hit, and sometimes not so much. But at the very least we can narrow down the type of firearms to look for from a crime scene."

I stand back, my brain still processing. "Thank you. That's really interesting. I learned about it in school, but it means so much more in real life."

A light bulb goes off in my head. "Do you do tire track comparisons, too?"

Justice Levi smiles. "Oh yes, that and shoe prints, tool mark comparisons, pry marks, knives, and such things."

"I will need your expert opinion on something later." The thoughts of the oddly shaped pieces of dirt come to mind.

CHAPTER 6

It was a short week at work and after my travel the upcoming weekend is welcome. I spend the days lounging with my cats, cleaning, and sketching.

By Monday I am feeling refreshed and actually get to work on time: 8:00 exactly. Woo-hoo! Inside I wave to my office mates as I walk by. When I get to my office, Patrick is sitting in his chair—another surprise that he is here and not in the back, and staring at his computer. His hands are not at the keyboard. He doesn't seem to notice my entrance.

"Hey Patrick, feeling better?"

He startles out of his trance. "Better—what do you mean?" His voice has an edge.

I am a bit taken aback at his tone. "Weren't you off sick Friday? Sorry."

"Oh yeah, right. Just taking care of my son. He had a stomach bug, thanks." He has two sons, and I know that one of them has some congenital heart problems. That's a great deal to worry about. Patrick looks sick, pale, and there is sheen of moisture on his skin. I don't want to get anywhere near those germs.

"Well, you better take care of yourself, too. I hope you didn't get sick from him," I say and sit down quietly and check my e-mails. I didn't find anything in my queue that needs my immediate attention. I walk up to the front office to say a proper good morning to the ladies. Doug is leaning over Mary Lou's desk, flirting, so I know it has to be a quiet day.

"Good morning." Mary Lou says with her usual warm smile.

"Thanks, good to know. How many today?" I look at Doug.

A crooked smile creeps over his face. "Only one. And Matt is doing it with Dr. Reeves." He is relishing his one-case day, as he should. It is a rare thing when this happens. "But it is a big one."

"What do you mean?"

Doug's chortling reddens his fair complexion. "Go on in the back and take a look."

My curiosity grows and I hurry back to the morgue.

As soon as I push through the double doors, I know something unusual has happened. Instead of two people working over the body in an otherwise empty room, there are four men in black suits hovering around the body, closely guarding the proceedings. Standing a few feet behind them is another man in a shirt and tie and gray pants, with his badge shining brightly on his belt. He is clearly not part of the group. I have met him before, a friendly detective from the Fairfax County Police. Detective Nguyen.

I walk over to him. "What's up?"

He nods toward the body. "Go take a look first."

I do as he says and make my way through the crowd of people. There lying on the gurney is an overweight, balding white man. His face is reddish purple and he has a silk scarf around his neck. He is wearing a pink angora sweater, pink pumps, and a pink miniskirt. None of the pinks match. Wow.

I walk back to Detective Nguyen. I am partial to him since he is of Vietnamese descent and I am half Japanese-Brazilian. There are not too many people of Asian descent around, and in a mostly subconscious way he is reassuring to me. I stand next to him and he leans toward me.

"He was DoD." Department of Defense. This revelation takes a moment to sink in. "Hence," he said, "all the suits."

It turns out to be the first autoerotic asphyxia death I have seen. We learned about them in school but I never expected to see one, much less a high-ranking federal employee. Apparently the sensation of an orgasm is enhanced when the brain is deprived of oxygen. In my pathology class, I learned it is a somewhat common practice for people to do this, mostly men, straight men, men I would never expect to dress up to masturbate.

Usually it is a man, not a woman, who will dress in women's clothing, or set up pictures of pornographic material within in their view. Then set up a ligature system that has a "safety" mechanism to allow them to release the choking ligature easily. But sometimes they pass out before changing position or the fail-safe fails and they end up dying via asphyxia.

"Wow." I am flabbergasted.

Detective Nguyen says, "I'm sure glad I'm not doing that notification. All the black suits are here to make sure the guy wasn't murdered and set up. I was at the scene; it seems like this behavior was a habit for him. He had all the gear and the porn. Lived alone. I'm just glad I'm not telling his old man what happened and having to explain the circumstances to him."

I completely agree with that.

The more time I spend in this field, the more I feel my perspective shifting. I have started seeing all the strange and depraved things that people do to one another and themselves.

I was first attracted to the work and pursued my degree in forensics because I wanted to help society. To learn how to figure out what happened at a scene and find the truth and help people and the justice system. It was a noble cause. My family wondered why I would want to do such work, but I knew that I wanted to do something with a greater meaning. Even if it is to help clean up the debris left from people's messy lives.

I don't bother to stay around for the autopsy for this one. It is obvious that the feds in the black suits prefer to keep things private. So I go to my office to work on some reports and paperwork from the recent cases.

I make a conscious effort to stay detached from the results of the daily suffering in people's lives that I see at the morgue. When people ask me how I deal with interacting with dead people all the time, I answer that since they are dead, they are not suffering anymore, so I know they are released from any pain. If I had to watch someone in pain like in an emergency room or be a nurse administering to suffering people, that's something I could not handle. The dead, they are easy, they are at peace—I hope. Or, at least they are no longer in pain.

I admit there have been individual cases that got to me. Last month a body came in to the office of a thirty-seven-year-old white male, good-looking and otherwise healthy man, who had killed himself. He had overdosed on pain medication intentionally and was found in his home by a neighbor. He'd left a suicide note that was over ten pages long. I had to read those pages, and the unnecessary suffering seeped deep into my psyche. All the pain he experienced in his childhood had never left him. He wrote how his father had always told him how bad and ugly he was. He said that he couldn't keep those words from echoing through his head every day. *Dad, you told me I was never good enough. A burden, ugly and stupid.* Even though he was in his thirties, he still felt like that small child being told how bad he was.

It saddens me to see how people use words without understanding their effect on others, especially their own children. The ones they are supposed to protect. But usually parents are where the deepest wounds come from. Clearly not everyone should be a parent.

The pain that a parent can inflict on a child with just a few words is immense. The man lying on the morgue table was not ugly; not by any stretch on the imagination. But according to his suicide note, he felt like the most repulsive human being around. I am guessing that he thought the pain would go away as he got older and he would forget. The fact was that he hadn't figured out how to move past or release the pain, and it was just too much for him to continue living. He looked like an adult on the outside, but the feeling of still being that scolded little boy on the inside was too much.

I feel so frustrated by the nonchalant way people raise their kids. When a person has a child, they forget how a parent is like a god to that child. Every kind word, smile, playtime shows the child how life is good and they are good. Every disparaging, angry, fearful word shows the child how life is bad and scary. Reading that suicide note made a wash of sadness rush over me, and tears well in my eyes.

In my mind, the goal of raising a child is to create a fully functioning, independent adult. It doesn't seem like that is what other people think or what the media sells. I have heard so many people say they want babies. But a baby is only a baby for so long, and then it becomes a toddler, then a child, a teenager, and hopefully an adult. I have seen people forget that a baby is not an accessory.

I had been so upset that day that I wanted to talk about it, and did so with Justice Levi Ferguson. He was typing at his computer and gave me his smile that lit up the room when I approached. His presence already comforting me.

"Can I come in for a bit?"

"Of course." He nodded at the chair on the other side of the desk. I sat and recounted the suicide case to him and could feel the moisture in my eyes coming back.

"Yes. Sad, indeed." He resonant voice soothed me. "I don't know why people lose faith. I have seen and felt a lot of the cruelty in the world, but the worst is when it comes from a family member. This society of ours makes us believe that our families should be the most kind and supportive aspect of our lives. But in truth, I have seen the worst cruelty come from those who are supposed to be the most supportive. Parents to children, husbands and wives. Sad."

He shook his head and looked at the pictures of his family decorating his desk. "That's why I've always endeavored to be kind to my wife and teach love rather than fear to my children." A picture of him and his wife and son and daughter, all with big, genuine smiles, stared back at him. His wife: pretty, with short blonde hair and a big smile. His son had a dark skin tone and was tall and fit, and his daughter with lighter skin and long dark hair. "Don't forget that there are good people out there, too," he said. "Your job is helping them in their time of despair, when they need assistance and compassion from their governmental agencies."

I always feel reassured when hearing his perspective. He has shown a protective streak with me, and he has warned me against being too open with people at work. I am still trying to learn how to do that as well as whom to trust. Justice, with over twenty years of experience playing politics on the state and county level, is still a kind and wise man, a survivor—as an African-American man in Virginia, especially in law enforcement. We have bonded over discussions of the meaning of life several times since I began working here. He is somewhat of a father figure to me. Not having had a positive, stable male role model and no real examples of lasting love, I find him reassuring.

Yeah, yeah, I know, I probably have daddy issues, but who doesn't? If it it's not daddy issues, then it's mommy issues.

After my parents' divorce, my father went off to unknown places and my mother continued her career as a translator. My grandmother was the only one in my family who I remember smiling often, but in the style of a typical old-world Japanese culture, we did not talk too much of emotions. She stayed with me while my older sister chose to go with my father and his new family to places far away, wherever he was stationed at the time. So my life was filled with a lot of silence, love from my cats, and the quiet humming of my grandmother. None of us have ever learned to speak the language of feelings. But then again, who really has?

The day progresses quietly. Patrick is still in a foul mood but I just try to ignore it. From the office gossip chain, I know he has a lot going on. He has a wife with health problems and two teenage young boys to care for. I can't even imagine that kind of pressure.

I try not to pry too much into his personal life. Later in the day, I see a note he left on my computer monitor saying that he had to leave early. It says he has some "family issues" to take care of. So I have the office to myself and turn on the radio to some upbeat music. Another e-mail from Dr. Cuezze comes in:

How about Sunday? I miss the museums, would you like to join me there?

He attached a comic image of a human staring at a statue of a Neanderthal. Very cute.

I quickly reply:

I love museums. Sounds great. I guess that means the Natural History?

I do a quick search and find an image of a sketch of a skull and attach it to the e-mail. I can't help but smiling. I wonder if he is as handsome in real life as in his photographs. I do another search for his name on the Internet. Images of him working at the World Trade Center on 9/11 come up, looking over remains at what is labeled "Aircraft crash victims still being identified." Wow, impressive. He has done a lot. I can't wait.

At 3:00 p.m., Lisa sticks her head in my door. I guess the front desk staff let her in. She is here often enough, and in the front office, Mary Lou and Betty recognize her.

"Hey man." She plops down in the wooden chair in front of my desk.

"What's up?" She always has some great stories. It amazes me what some police officers go through on a day-to-day basis.

"What. A. Day." She props her feet up on an unoccupied corner of my desk, her heavy black boots almost blocking my view of her face. "I pulled over this guy who had been driving up and down the highway and flashing his penis at women who drove by." She shakes her head. "People are crazy."

I have to laugh. "Wow. What did he say when you pulled him over?"

She leans toward me and a grin creeps across her face and her green eyes glint. "He said he forgot his pants!" She bursts out into a hysterical laughter that is contagious. I break into a giggle then a full-blown cackle.

After wiping tears from her eyes, she straightens her face and gets serious. "Sorry, I'm still tired. Anyway, we got some news about my guy."

"My guy?"

"The death in the car the other day."

"Oh yeah." It's hard for me to keep track of all the bodies. "What did you find out?"

"He was involved in a lot of bad stuff before he went to jail. And no one seemed to really like him, not even his own sister, according to the officer, although I want to go and talk to her myself." She looks up at me. "Do you want to go with me? Now?"

"I would love to, but let me ask Dr. Reeves. It is a little unusual." That would be a first for me, to interview a family member in person.

"Let me go and ask her, it will seem more official." Lisa stands up and straightens her uniform and heads back to Dr. Reeves's office before I can say anything.

In a few minutes Lisa is back. "It's cool with her. It is, after all, almost the end of the day."

I look at my watch and realize that it is already 3:30.

"Let's drop your car at the apartment, as it's on the way," Lisa suggests, "and we can take mine over there."

That makes sense to me, considering the hour we will get caught up in traffic one way or another.

By the time we get to my apartment complex, Lisa has moved the arm for the laptop that all police cars have and I just have enough room to fit in. We head down Route 236 to Dumfries, a small in-between town that is surprisingly rural for being so close to the U.S. capital.

The green-and-brown hills roll by as we leave Fairfax county (I know this by the signs on the street) and pass through the city of Manassas, then head south where there are fewer and fewer buildings and lots of lush grass and trees. The dogwoods and cherry blossoms are pushing out their beautiful white and pink blossoms. I tell her about my Roanoke case and a little about Dr. Cuezze. But I don't want to seem like I am too swept away. Not yet. I haven't even met him, but I definitely feel drawn to him.

Lisa continues about the case at hand. "Robert Greeley was a contractor, divorced and both his parents are dead, looks like legal next of kin is his sister, Donna Wright, since his kids are underage."

"Donna's husband is one John Wright, and he is on disability now. He was a real estate developer and brought them up to northern Virginia when he was healthy, but then got hurt doing work on the renovation in Chinatown in D.C. and had to go on disability. So work dried up for Robert."

I notice Donna's address and phone number. That's funny—it's the same phone number as my mom's, just with a different area code.

"What is Donna doing for work?" I ask.

"It looks like she had to get a job as an office assistant in Woodbridge." Lisa is paging back and forth between documents. "Not making the big bucks, and a lot of mouths to feed." She adjusts her heavy belt as she is driving.

We pull into a trailer park that looks like it was built in the 1970s. The outside of Donna Wright's trailer is tidy, small, and pink with light-gray shutters. Lisa finds a way to park among the small winding roads, and we get out.

Lisa approaches the door and knocks. A Ford Taurus, based on the way it's parked, looks like it belongs to this residence.

A dishwater-blonde woman opens the door. She is wiry thin and wearing a T-shirt and sweatpants.

"Can I help you?" She has a scowl on her face, with a hint of distrust. I don't take it personally, as I'm sure no one is ever happy to see the police at their door.

Lisa goes into cop mode. "Yes ma'am. I am Officer Byrd and this is Investigator Rawson, and we're here to ask you a couple of questions about your brother, Robert."

"Come in," she sighs and steps away from the door. "There isn't much room, though."

When we enter I see that she is right; the three of us can barely fit into the cramped, narrow living room. It is tidy, though, and a galley kitchen that serves as a hallway leads to what looks like the other half of the trailer. The motif is orange and country kitsch.

"So what do you need to know?" She plops down into the arms of a faded, brown recliner. Lisa and I stay standing, even though there is a narrow yellow-fabric couch next to her, facing the small television.

"Was your brother living with you?" Lisa asks. As far as I am concerned, I am just here to observe.

"Just for the last few weeks. Since he got out of jail." Her eyes are red rimmed. "He was a jackass but not a mean guy."

I look around the trailer and notice five medication bottles lined up on the coffee table in front of the TV.

"Do you live alone, Mrs. Wright?" Lisa asks, also looking around.

"No, my husband is in the back, asleep." She motions to the rooms beyond the kitchen. "He was in an accident a few years back and has been on disability since. The medications knock him out." She is fumbling with a pen while she talks and starts to cough. She continues to hack, and Lisa and I look at each other.

"Can we get you something?" I ask, alarmed. Donna Wright shakes her head and fumbles for the drawer next to her chair. She pulls out an asthma inhaler and sucks in deep breaths. Her body relaxes and she leans back, silent again.

"Can you get me some water, please?" She looks at me with large and watery eyes.

I take a few steps and am in the small kitchen, where I find a green plastic cup in the drying rack. I fill it with tap water and take it to her.

She drinks the water in one gulp and is breathing again normally. "I have asthma, and it sneaks up on me." She leans back. "That's what smoking three packs a day for fifteen years does."

A noise comes from the other side of the trailer. "You okay?" comes a muffled man's voice through the wall.

"I'm fine," Donna yells back. "The cops are here about Robert."

A minute later a very large man appears at the door. He can barely squeeze through the hallway. He clearly was once a big man, and his over six-foot height is stooped over and cushioned by his large stomach. I am sure that isn't helping his back problems.

Lisa holds her hat tighter in her hands. "Mr. Wright, we're just here to ask you and your wife about your brother-in-law."

He pushes his disheveled hair back from his face. "Well, not much to say. He was here for a few weeks while he looked for work when he wasn't down trying to visit his kids. He could still do construction and I was trying to find him some work, but I've been out of the business for a while." He makes his way to the couch and falls down into the cushions.

"Do you know of any enemies that your brother may have?" Lisa is still looking around, and the space is feeling smaller and smaller.

"We don't know about his friends, if he has any around here anymore." Donna looks at her husband. "I can't think of anyone who would want to hurt him."

"Anyone from his old work, or that you can think of?" Lisa looks at John.

He pauses to think. "His ex would bring the kids up to visit him in Coffeewood every six months. I don't know much else; he was in for seven years and we could only see him a few times a year. It isn't exactly close by."

We nod; the correctional facility is about an hour away, and this couple doesn't seem to be any shape to travel.

Donna speaks again. "I signed the paperwork for the funeral home, but his ex-wife, Tina, and her kids are going to take care of the arrangements. I guess things between them weren't too bad. I never liked her though, always thought she deserved more than she would work for."

"Well, thank you for your time." Lisa pulls out a business card and offers it to Donna, who continues to sit.

"We'll let ourselves out."

Lisa and I get back into her cruiser and sit in silence for a moment. She speaks first. "What a life."

"I know. They don't look like they're in any shape to have been involved in the murder."

"I would have to agree. They certainly could not have pulled off something like that themselves. And the sister didn't even ask about any insurance, so it doesn't look like she'll be getting anything. Or is interested." Lisa pulls out into the heavy traffic back to take me home.

"I'm hungry. You want to eat?" I ask.

She glances at me. "Of course." Cops and food, they always go together. "You know of any good place?"

I pause and mine the menu in my brain. There are so many restaurants in this part of Virginia but only a few are of note. "There's a little sushi place up the road."

"Sounds good, better than sitting in this traffic."

We find our way to a small restaurant in a strip mall and get settled in. Lisa has brought her file with her. "I was intrigued by Robert because he looked familiar to me and I couldn't figure out why. I've been working some cold cases recently, and in one of the files I saw this composite sketch. A pretty good sketch, drawn by hand." She pulls a folded piece of paper out of her pocket and unfolds it. "See, it looks like the guy, huh?"

The paper she put in front of me is a photocopy of a sketch of the face of a white male with longish hair, pulled back into a ponytail as well as a photocopy of Robert Greeley's driver's license. He has an elongated head shape and small eyes. It does look similar to the man we pulled out of the car the other night, but younger. "What year is this from?"

"Nineteen ninety-four, so take off eight years from the guy and I think it looks pretty similar. He was a suspect for a robbery."

I study Robert Greeley's face that I have in the file on my desk. The pencil lines in Lisa's sketch depict a thin face, beaklike nose, and ponytail. His eyes stare out at the viewer. The face shape, eyes, and nose are very similar to the driver's license photograph. I can definitely see the resemblance.

"Close . . . not a bad sketch. Who did it? Are they still around?"

"It was a Great Falls Police Department case, but the guy who did the drawing was out of Prince William PD, he's a captain now but was a detective at the time, I think. We still have this image because we thought it was related to some robberies done on the highway. I met the artist in a blood spatter analysis class last year, funny guy. Maybe I'll give him a call and see if he thinks if the dead guy looks like our guy. I'm going to head home to Stephanie for my days off. I'll do it when I get back and let you know what else comes up."

"Why don't you give me the artist's phone number and I'll call him while you're off? Maybe I can set something up by the time you're back." I'm getting interested now.

"Sounds good to me." She searches through her pile of files, finds the number, and writes it down on a Post-it Note for me.

I examine the bright-pink piece of paper. The name "Francisco Garcia" is scribbled in letters above a 703 area code phone number. "I guess he's not from around here?"

"I dunno, from one of the islands or something. Cuba, Puerto Rico, something . . . nice guy."

I am excited to talk to someone who does composite sketches. A few months after I started working here, I had the opportunity to take a class with the National Center for Missing & Exploited Children, or NCMEC, to create postmortem images to aid in identifying nameless decedents. This skill is helpful for our office, too, since it can give names to the unidentified bodies that occasionally come in.

NCMEC was started by John Walsh, the father of a missing child, to help find missing kids. He became an advocate for victims and their families, and with others lobbied Congress to create NCMEC in 1984. Sadly, John Walsh's son was later found murdered.

NCMEC creates most of the age-progressed images of children that are on the back of milk cartons and fliers. The organization also offers training for law enforcement and other government workers on how to create forensic images. Their headquarters is in Alexandria, Virginia, only a few miles from my office, so I was able to take the free training thanks to my affiliation with the Medical Examiner's Office.

Lisa and I eat dinner and relax as much as we can with her in uniform. People in restaurants always go on high alert when someone in uniform is there. By the time we finish dinner, the traffic has settled down some. Then we make our way back to Burke.

In the car Lisa switches on the radio, and National Public Radio is playing. The news announces that we are on Yellow Alert today. Since 9/11 feelings of insecurity still permeate our everyday life, especially in the Washington D.C. metro area. The media makes it worse by inundating us with how stressed out we should feel, red being the highest and yellow for less stressed. There have been reports about how to create a safety package to store in our homes, just in case. They recommend that everyone have a kit filled with food, maps, extra clothing, duct tape, and much more at the ready to take with us when we flee the area. On the highways digital banners tell us what cars to look out for—one of those might be a terrorist. We are constantly reminded to be on the lookout for something or other. I switch off the radio. I want to feel peaceful, not stressed out.

The shock and devastation of the 9/11 events still resonate loudly here. I remember being at home that day in McLean, only three miles from downtown D.C. and five from the Pentagon, sitting in front of the TV watching the planes crash into the towers in New York City. Like everyone else, I was frozen in disbelief and horror. After seeing so many TV and movie images of imaginary events like this, it was hard to believe this one was real. It happened before I started my job at the Medical Examiner's office, and I was so frustrated to sit and watch and not be able to help.

When the reality of the events sank in, I scrambled to call friends and family who lived in New York City. For hours all I could get was a busy signal, but I eventually spoke to the people I knew living there. Thankfully they were safe, unlike so many others.

A couple of weeks after 9/11, I drove by the Pentagon, and the huge crater in the building was visible from the road. The sight shook me to the core. The American paradigm that we live in a bubble of safety had violently burst.

"Always so cheerful," Lisa says and turns off the radio. We drive the rest of the way pondering in silence. I know Lisa is eager to drop me off to get on her way to Steph, and I always like time at home alone. As a true introvert, I need my time alone to rejuvenate.

CHAPTER 7

The next morning Patrick is back in the office, and we only have two bodies for autopsies. He takes one and I the other. By 10:00 I am back up front at my desk and delighted to find that I have another e-mail from Michael Cuezze:

Great. Looking forward to it. How about we meet at the museum? How does 10am sound?"

I smile and type back:

Sounds great. See you soon! Then I list my cell phone number.

I let myself daydream about him for a moment and then focus on what is in front of me. When done with my paperwork, I decide to give the composite artist guy, Francisco Garcia, a call.

"Garcia." A resonant, clear voice comes through after the second ring.

I explain who I am and why I am calling. "Interesting," he responds. I can detect a slight accent. After a pause he says, "I do remember those robberies; they were a big deal at the time. Sure, I've gotta go up to the lab, anyway, I'll stop by after."

"Sounds good, thank you so much. See you soon."

Wow, I am happy for the quick response.

I pull out the case file Lisa gave me about the man found in the car: Robert Greeley. The file includes his prior arrests for a string of burglaries; nothing too successful. All arrests were made by the

Prince William County Police Department. Interesting.

Technically the duties as a Medicolegal Death Investigator are limited to assisting in the determination of the cause and manner of death, not to catch the bad guys. But it is hard not to get interested in finding out what happened in certain cases, especially when the investigator is a friend. This case is unusual and the suspect is still out there, piquing my curiosity.

Mary Lou's voice comes through the speaker on my desk phone. "Someone here to see you." I can also hear the echo of her real voice coming from the other room; she is only about twenty feet away. Expecting the sketch artist, I walk the few steps to the front door, which is also code locked, and let him in.

He is an attractive man with dark-chocolate colored hair in a short, military-style haircut, dressed as most detectives in a button-down shirt, tie, slacks, and, of course, sensible shoes. He stands about six-foot tall with a build that still reflects his time, I am guessing, in the military service.

"Hey, I'm Francisco Garcia." He smiles and reaches out his hand. We quickly shake hands then step into my office.

"I'm Julia Rawson. Thanks for coming in. Lisa Byrd says hello, by the way." I sit down and he takes the lone hard chair facing my desk.

"Oh great, she was a lot of fun. Tell her I said hey."

I've learned that it's always a good idea to name drop with law enforcement. They determine a lot by knowing whom a person is friendly with. And, as in all groups, there are those who like one another and those who definitely do not.

Francisco and I fall into chitchat; he talks about how he came from south Florida and stayed here after his Navy service, about his wife and three sons. Then we get to business.

"So what's this case of mine you wanted to ask about?"

I pull out the file and show him the copy of the composite sketch. He takes the paper from me and looks at the pencil drawing of the man with the long face and scraggly hair staring back at him.

"Yeah, I vaguely remember doing that sketch. It was a long time ago but the witness was really good." He keeps staring at the image, squinting as he tries to recall the details. "Yeah, yeah. The witness was from the house next door and saw this guy coming out of the house that was broken into when he was walking his dog." Francisco nods vigorously. "The witness described the guy really well. He was a retired FBI agent and seemed to have excellent recall." He looks up at me and hands the page back. "What happened with him?"

I pass him the autopsy photograph of the decedent from the car accident scene. "This is the man who I thought looks like your sketch. If it's the same man, then I thought your case might have something to do with his death." The image is a close-up image of Greeley's face. The muscles are relaxed and his jaw is slack, but we had cleaned up the dried blood and pushed back his hair so you could see his features.

Francisco scans the photo. "Yeah, there are definite similarities. We could ask the witness if it matters." He glances up at me. "Can I keep this?"

"Sure." I give him the rundown on what we know so far about Robert Greeley.

He smiles and leans back. "I was a homicide detective at the time, but I do composites for our department as well as surrounding agencies as a courtesy. I wear a lot of hats." He chuckles. "I remember there were several robberies in the fancy houses in Great Falls, then we got some in Prince William, and that's when we got Greeley. But it was never proven that he was associated with the Great Falls cases. I guess I wasn't on those robberies. I just did the sketch for this one."

Patrick breezes into the office and pauses when he sees an unusual visitor. He does the cop nod to Francisco; they can recognize each other through "copdar." Francisco stands and proffers his hand. Patrick stares at it momentarily, then forces a smile and shakes it.

"Francisco Garcia." I notice he does not use his title. That is unusual for a police officer. Police departments are paramilitary organizations, and most cops are quite attached to their rank. I am impressed that Francisco does not lord his captaincy over Patrick.

"Patrick McConnell." Patrick stands taller. "I think we may have met when I was a detective with Great Falls PD."

Francisco nods. "Yeah, okay. How are you doing?"

They fall into a cop-dance that I am just learning about. How police officers size each other up. The process creates an interesting and somewhat humorous dynamic. Almost like watching predators in nature, like in the TV show *Wild Kingdom.*

"Well, I got to go and help Mary Lou, she needs me to get her some info." Patrick steps over to his desk and grabs some papers, gives the cop nod, and leaves the office.

Francisco sits down again. "Yeah, I remember him." He takes a deep breath and I think he is going to say something else, but he keeps quiet. "Anyway, I'll let you know if I can get in touch with the witness. It won't be enough to close the case, but it will give me some peace of mind."

I stand to thank him and ask that he let me know anything else that comes up.

He rises and extends his hand again in parting. "Okay, now the wait begins." We shake hands again and he leaves to go to the laboratory upstairs.

A few minutes later, Patrick returns to the office. He looks around. "That detective gone? What was that all about?"

I nod and fill him in about the Greeley case, suddenly realizing I haven't asked him about this case at all. I haven't seen him much since that death occurred.

He shrugs, turning his back to look at paperwork on his desk. "I don't really remember that too much."

Okay. That seems odd. I drop it—obviously he has a lot on his mind. When I first started at this job, I learned from my other coworkers that his wife had been diagnosed with cancer last year and his son has a congenital heart problem. But we never talk about it. So I don't push.

Back when I started, Patrick took me under his wing. He was patient and tried to show me the ropes in the office. He was usually friendly when we were alone, but whenever anyone else was around he seemed to lose interest. It is a strange relationship; I have become more independent and fostered relationships with the doctors and other police, as well as other coworkers in the office. Perhaps he thinks I've betrayed him.

I'm not sure if he resents that I have stopped relying on him so much, but that's the way things go. Just like when I entered a new grade in school; usually the first friends you make are not the ones you stick with.

At the end of the day, I leave the building right on time. I decide to treat myself to some Indian food for dinner. I call in my order to my favorite restaurant, Minerva: chicken tikka masala with garlic naan bread. Yum.

At home I eat in front of the television watching nothing in particular, and savoring the flavorful food. The cats are not interested in tonight's meal; too spicy for their liking. After some relaxing I take a shower and settle into my queen-size bed under the down comforter with the two cats joining me for treats and cuddles. A wonderful reprieve from the rest of the world and one of my favorite spots on earth: in my bed with my cats.

CHAPTER 8

The next morning I'm in the morgue trotting from one examination area to the next taking photographs and climbing up and down the mobile stairs. I don't notice Rick until he is just below me at the foot of the short ladder.

"Hey Jules!" he calls up to me.

He is standing there in his dark-blue uniform, smiling, with a big folder of papers in his hand.

"Hey!" I almost fall off when I look down. I smile nervously and grip the metal rail with one hand and the camera in my latex-gloved hands while gingerly backing down the wobbly steps.

"What's up?" I remove the camera that was strapped around my neck and place it on the small rolling table beside the body laid out on the metal gurney.

We walk over to the side of the room as the air fills with the whine of the autopsy saw used to cut through the cranium to remove the brain. I wave Rick toward the door that leads into the offices and remove my protective gear.

We push through the two sets of double doors into what seems like silence for the first instant. The buzzing sound behind us quiets. As we enter my office, Rick drops the folder on my desk.

"What's this?" I am exhausted and a little sore from standing over the three bodies that had come in during the evening before; I am the only person helping in the back other than Matt, who is notorious for doing as little as possible.

"It's stuff about the guy in the car we found, Robert Greeley. I just got the records from the Fishersville PD. It took them a while, but I think the department is pretty small and likely understaffed."

I sit down at my desk, glancing at the workspace next to me and seeing that it's empty. Mental note: Patrick wasn't in the lab and he's not at his desk, either.

"What did you find?" I ask Rick. I don't feel like looking at the files at that moment; in reality it isn't our job to investigate the crime, just determine cause and manner of death based on evidence found at the scene and from the body. We are reminded of this often by other police officers. Of course, we determine the type of death they're investigating, so the reasoning is somewhat circular, but it's all done in cooperative manner. Rick and Lisa are the only ones who completely share information with me and are genuinely interested in my impressions. I have been learning more and more how important personal relationships are at work; it makes all the difference in being successful and, frankly, happy at the job. And you never know whose help you may need one day, so never burn your bridges. Justice Ferguson has told me on several occasions, "Watch how you treat people; you never know who will end up your boss."

"Well," Rick says, "he got into a lot of trouble in Fishersville when he was there. His family probably doesn't know it, but he has a $250,000 life insurance policy on him that was initiated last week. We're still waiting to see the details of the policy; beneficiaries and the like."

"When Lisa and I met with his sister and brother-in-law, they didn't seem like they were in shape to do anything physical." I recall her asthmatic breathing and his obvious physical disability. "Didn't you say that he has kids? They or their mother probably get it."

"We'll let you know when we get that paperwork." Rick settles into the chair in front of my desk, and I proceed to be inundated with stories of his ex-wife and his two kids who are now grown. There are always stories. It's true that being married to a cop is tough. Rick allegedly isn't a cheater, but the instability of any sort of schedule is hard for some women to get used to, and the women who are attracted to them, "badge bunnies," are not the most stable people, either. I have heard crazy stories about women throwing themselves at cops when they were pulled over. Or after they get a cop's card and then start calling him to the point of stalking. It is almost as bad as the women who start writing to criminals in jail stating their undying love to them or a desire to bear their children.

I have dated a few people in my life, mostly disappointments. Then met someone I thought I would be with for a while: Victor. He was tall and pleasant enough to date long distance, as he lived in Boston and I in northern Virginia. But when I stayed with him for my internship, it was not as good as I had hoped. We had a whirlwind romance and marriage, many travel adventures, but the lack of communication made me feel even more alone than when I was single. I didn't feel connected. He wanted to go the traditional route—marriage, house, and two kids. Exactly what I don't want. Although I had told him that before I moved in, he said that he thought I would "change my mind." I knew I wouldn't and didn't want to be with someone who didn't respect my desires, and clearly had different ones for life.

I have always wanted to find a partner, and at the same time the idea of kids always repelled me. When the other girls in school were playing with dolls, I was playing with animals or cars. It never occurred to me to have children. I have been told by lots of strangers that I would change my mind when I hit twenty-five or thirty, or more. But it still hasn't happened yet at age twenty-seven, if anything the desire to not have children has gotten stronger. I would never do a child the disservice of having a parent who doesn't really want them. I equate having a child to going to medical school. It takes many years to get through, is very expensive, a lifetime commitment, a title you will always have, as well as holding the fate of another's life in your own hands. I definitely think it is not a decision to be made lightly.

I broke up with Victor because I knew that he would find some woman who wanted exactly what he wanted. It wasn't easy, but I'm glad that I stayed true to myself about what I do and don't want. I wouldn't be persuaded to make a life-changing decision that would affect not only two adults, but also any children that came into our lives. So we parted ways.

In my family of origin (that's therapist-speak) my parents didn't do positive relationship well, so I don't know what that even looks like. I was six years old when my parents decided to give up on pretending we were a family.

My parents met in Brazil when my father was in the Peace Corps. He had been inspired by John F. Kennedy's speech and joined the Corps when Kennedy established it by executive order in March 1961. His job as a twenty-year-old with an associate's degree was to help develop an irrigation system for the town where I would be born. A big responsibility; I can't even imagine.

My mother was young and beautiful, petite with long black hair, and the only person who knew how to speak any English in the town. Her parents came from Japan in the 1920s and had built up a good family name, reputation, and worth. Brazil has the largest Japanese population outside of Japan itself, a group that started migrating to Brazil in the 1920s. My mother always had an aptitude for language and she wanted to use it as her ticket out of the small town where she grew up. She married my father when they were only twenty-one.

After seventeen years, mostly filled with disappointed silences and never any fun or laughter that I could remember, they went their separate ways. My father went back into a job that took him overseas and my mother to a translation job that took her all over the world often and for long periods. She had never wanted children, and I knew that having a family was a burden to her. She, like so many other women in the 1960s and before, married and had children to fulfill their duty, no matter what her personal preferences were. I didn't want to do the same.

I listened to Rick and then gave him a hug before he left. I am curious to see what Robert Greeley's insurance policy says, and who the beneficiaries are, or who are not. Isn't it funny how family is always the prime suspect in a murder?

CHAPTER 9

That evening I am home sitting on my back porch enjoying the fresh air of the warm day and the view of the trees that abut the apartment. The apartments in my complex are "garden style." I don't know exactly what that means, but the layout is a two-level above ground, with one apartment below. They are about thirty years old, with nondescript vinyl siding. They are the only apartments in Burke, surrounded by townhouses and single-family homes.

My porch is standard apartment issue, but I've made it friendly with herbs and some minor landscaping. Given my propensity for moving around since college, I consider it a good effort at hominess. I am considering what to eat for dinner when there is a knock at my front door. I move to the door, open it, and find Lisa standing there with a big grin holding a paper grocery bag.

"I found some fresh salmon at the store—it's in season." She raises the bags as she walks in. We have found that we both love to cook, so that is something we share often.

There is a small forest next to the apartment that my balcony overlooks. It is relaxing to have nature so close, and in the middle of such a large metropolitan area. Sometimes at night I can even hear the foxes scream. The first time I have ever heard one it sounded like a wounded woman and scared the crap out of me.

Lisa settles down on one of the two stools in front of the counter that opens between the kitchen and the dining room. She is out of uniform, which always comes as a surprise to me. She is wearing boot-cut jeans and a black button-down shirt with a skull design on it. Her hair is down, lying in pretty blonde waves that come naturally from her Swedish heritage, enhanced by the salon.

"Steph is working on this awesome mural for Smokey's Restaurant, and she also needs to work on another project, so I decided to head back early and hang out." Her girlfriend, Stephanie, is a mural painter and woodworker. She recently got a contract with a local restaurant chain to do the fantastic murals that cover the walls of their many restaurants.

"Since you're here, why don't you take a look at these." I pass her the files that Rick gave me. I planned on looking through them tonight.

"I haven't gotten a chance to look at these yet since I was off," Lisa says. She spreads the files out on the table and starts reading while I make dinner. "Richard Thomas Greeley, born February 11, 1954 in Fishersville, Virginia, went to Fishersville High School, spent a year at Blue Ridge Community College studying to be an electrician. He was in Fishersville doing odd jobs until 1990, when he came to northern Virginia." She pages through more files. "He was married in 1980 to a Kristy Wetfield and had two kids. Divorced in 1995 after he went to jail. I guess that's another reason why he moved up to this region, too. His kids are eleven and thirteen—both boys, Ryan and Kyle."

I add the sauce to the salmon before putting it into the oven to bake. I also decide to prepare some green beans with garlic (garlic, always a necessity when cooking), olive oil, and crushed red peppers and put them in the oven. Yum. "So where's the ex-wife now?"

Lisa hums while she turns through more pages. Simon is circling her feet, as he knows that when Lisa's over that means food. She likes to feed him scraps, and he particularly likes fish. Kudo is not fussy and never eats human food, so is relaxing in a ball on the futon couch. She looks like a fuzzy caterpillar when she sits like that.

Lisa says, "It looks like the ex and kids are in Staunton."

I join her at the table with glasses of ice water for each of us. Neither of us wants to drink alcohol, as we are both on call. We look through the papers together, still not seeing the answer.

I hear a pop from the oil in the pan and run back to stir the garlic around the salmon but am not really focused. My mind is trying to picture all the players and put them into some order. Who would want this man dead? And why?

"How are things at work? The anthropologist?" Lisa changes the subject as I put the food on the table and take a seat. "This is great, by the way," she says after her first mouthful of food.

I smile. "Thanks. He's coming to town and wants to meet up."

"Ooh, I can't wait to hear about it." She looks sideways at me. I can't stop the grin that comes over my face.

After Lisa leaves I spend the rest of the evening cleaning the apartment and feel accomplished.

CHAPTER 10

I get to the office the next day feeling refreshed after a full night's sleep with no interruptions. My red message light is shining when I get to work. I'm not sure who would have called me overnight; it was most likely a doctor or nurse for one of the recent cases. When I play the message, I hear, "Hey Julia, this is Michael Cuezze. I'm looking forward to seeing you on Sunday; here's my cell number if you need to reach me." He rattles off the number. "Have a great day."

I'm excited about meeting him in person and hopefully getting to spend some real time with him, and I love going downtown to the museums.

I smile and drift off for a moment, then gather myself into the present. There are three bodies in the morgue today, and I am working on gathering their medical records in my office when I hear the front door open and see Mary Lou go to the reception window. Usually it is someone delivering the mail, or from a funeral home, but this time her demeanor changes and she glances at me and waves me over.

I get up and approach the front window, where I see a pretty woman with strawberry-blonde hair and two boys with her complexion behind her. One is the same height as her, approximately five two, and the other stands just a bit taller. All are very thin, and the shorter boy is wearing thick, black-rimmed glasses.

"I am Kristy Greeley, Robert Greeley's wife, and these are his two kids, Ryan and Kyle." They look at me with wide eyes and make no movement.

Mary Lou steps away and lets me handle this. "Just a moment, ma'am, I'll be right out." I exit the secured area and go to the lobby so we can speak to each other without talking through glass.

"I am so sorry for your loss," I say. Having heard and said this statement time and time again in the outside corridors of the office, it seems like the right and only thing to say at this point. She nods and her pink lips tremble.

"It's been hard on the boys and me." She glances at them. Both dark haired and thin, they have already distracted themselves by each playing on a handheld video game. "Although maybe not too hard, since he's been in jail for so long." She sighs. "I was hoping he would get to see them more now that he's out."

"I met Donna, his sister, as we were under the impression that you are divorced, so legally she is the next of kin." I am afraid to broach this subject, but it is necessary.

Wendy shifts from one leg to the other. "Well, yes, we were divorced, but I still wanted to know. I couldn't believe it was him who died. I just want to see him before the funeral home takes him away."

This is always an uncomfortable situation. "Well, ma'am, I am sorry, but we are really not equipped to show you. It is best to have the funeral home show you." I don't know what else to say.

Unlike in TV and movies, we do not have a facility or the wherewithal to show families their loved ones. The funeral homes can clean up and present the bodies in ways we do not, so it's best that they show the body. We do not do visual identifications; we only accept them through scientific means, either fingerprints or DNA.

"They should be coming to get him today," I tell her. "I know that Donna just signed the paperwork. So you will be handling the arrangements, then?"

She nods and pulls out a tissue to dab at her eyes. "Well, okay. Will you tell them to call me when they get him? We are just up for the day, and I want to get home as soon as I can." She looks over at the boys. "We were down in Panama City, Florida, when we got the call. Visiting my cousin who lives there. We just drove straight here." She sighs and looks as exhausted as I imagine she is.

"Yes I will, ma'am. I am sorry that I couldn't help you more."

She nods and gathers the boys and heads out the door.

I feel her sadness and wish I could do more, but know that it would not be a good idea for her to see Robert right now.

I head back to my office and pick up the phone to call Lisa; she should know that it sounds like Robert Greeley's ex-wife was out of town when he died.

"Thanks for letting me know," Lisa says. "I will verify her alibi, but it sounds pretty tight. I'll talk to you in a couple of days."

After talking to Lisa, I put on my headphones and favorite music, and block out the sad thoughts that are accumulating in my head.

CHAPTER 11

Sunday finally comes and I am glad to go downtown to D.C., though I am feeling nervous and overwhelmed about meeting Michael. I had tried to stop myself from fantasizing, as that can always lead to a strange situation, but I couldn't help myself and had done just a little bit.

I drive to the closest Metro station, Vienna Metro, and park. It is the last station on the orange line headed west. I choose to take the Metro because it's just easier to not be tied down to a parking spot when wandering around D.C. Plus I don't know how long I will be there, and this seems like the easiest thing to do. The lot is mostly empty since it is Sunday and the commuters are at home.

I love going to downtown D.C. The energy is always so vibrant and optimistic. When I first moved to the area, I worked in a law firm and got to spend more time in town while getting my master's degree at George Washington University. So I know the area pretty well. Riding the Metro is so soothing to me. The sound of the trains thumping along, bright cars with clean orange-and-white seats, and the energy and excitement of the riders always bring a smile to my face. I just bought my twenty-five-year-anniversary Metro card; it is new and hard plastic that you can add money to, a new style as opposed to the easily degradable paper cards. Having a plastic card rather than a paper one that I can replenish makes me feel like a true D.C.-area resident.

Most of the riders who get on at each stop are obviously tourists—different people looking lost and excited to be in the capital and confused as which stop to get off for the monuments and attractions. There is one family in the same car as us, with the dad standing examining the Metro map on the inside wall, trying to navigate a simple rectangle that is bisected by the various trains deep under the ground. The apparent father of three small, blond children announces at every stop how many more there are to go. He has to rise from his seat several times to corral one or the other children from running up and down the car. The mother sits and watches, looking tired and pleased.

I get off at the stop for the Smithsonian and the National Mall. As I step off the Metro, I enter a man-made cement cave. The ceilings are at least fifty feet high, which gives a strangely open feeling, with a waffle like ceiling to collect the rising noises. I ride the steep tunnel escalator up, being reborn into the bright sunlight of the surface world.

Washington, D.C., is such a difference from where I grew up in a relatively rural part of New York, a small town with no curbs or sidewalks. D.C. is a place with so many interesting people, so diverse and exciting. I love that D.C. doesn't have the towering buildings of New York City, so there is no feeling of claustrophobia. The District has so many more flowers and trees, and is greener than New York, too, at least in the northwest quadrant where I was during school. I pride myself in having gotten to know the area by a lot of reading and studying maps, to finally become somewhat urban savvy.

I emerge onto the large green area of the National Mall, which is the original meaning of *mall*: a public area where people gather. I am in the northwest quadrant of the city, which has most of the tourist attractions, including the Smithsonian Institution's various museums—Natural History, The Castle, Air and Space, and American History—and the Washington Monument. A planned city, it has four quadrants, all originating from the Capitol Building. The numbered streets run north–south and the lettered streets east–west. Curiously, there is no J Street in any of the quadrants. The confusing streets are the ones named after states that radiate out of the parks and in all different directions.

I take a deep breath, trying to calm myself before meeting Michael. My feet crunch as I tread along the pebbled walkway of the mall; it is just starting to get more green than brown after the cold winter. There are a good number of people wandering around, as the weather is warming up. I look around, always having to admire the views: the majestic arch of the Capitol to one side and the towering Washington Monument to the other.

The National Museum of Natural History is one of the largest museums in the Smithsonian and certainly an imposing one. The large stone, Roman-style Corinthian columns stand at the top of massive steps. I always feel invigorated here, and eagerly enter through the front doors. Since 9/11, though, things have gotten scarier and the security even more paranoid, so I have to stand in line to have my bag looked through at security.

Once in the main room, I look at the towering elephant on his podium, his trunk held high in all his majestic glory. I glance at my watch, and note that it is 10:10 a.m.; I need to get better with the whole punctuality thing. I look around the crowds of people—it is always busy on the weekends—and recognize Dr. Cuezze from his picture. His back is to me, a slight but muscular frame wearing a black jacket, jeans, and cowboy boots. He looks around as I approach. His eyes twinkle and I can tell that he is pleased with what he sees in me. I am wearing my own black slacks, fitted red, merino wool sweater with my black Pea coat. I blush, and I am happy with the way he looks, too. His pictures didn't do him justice; plus I always find intelligence appealing.

I smile. "Hi, Dr. Cuezze, thank you so much for inviting me."

"Mike, please. None of this 'doctor' business; it sounds so formal. And thank you for coming out." He smiles warmly and reaches out his hand. We grasp hands for a few seconds longer than usual, his skin smooth and warm. His grip is strong but not overpowering.

He looks up at the pachyderm. "He's pretty impressive, isn't he?"

I turn and look at the elephant. "Yes, very."

"He's a fourteen-foot tall African elephant and was first put here in 1959. They have done their best to keep him looking good."

We walk slowly around the display. "He is impressive. How did you know all that?" I am intrigued.

"I did some research here for a paper I was writing, the anthropologists here are fellow University of Tennessee graduates so it was a lot of fun. I learned a lot and got to stay here a for a number of months."

"You went to the University of Tennessee?" Dork - I can hear the admiration in my own voice.

"Yes, and yes, I did study at the Body Farm with Bill Bass." I'm sure he gets that question all the time. Dr. Bill Bass is somewhat of a celebrity in the field. "At the University of Tennessee, we had these steam-jacketed vats housed at the vet school. They're the same kind that the Navy uses for cooking large meals on ships. Steam is released at uniform levels and is very good at rendering bone; nothing like evenly distributed heat to clean bone. You just have to keep an eye on it or else the steam will dry out in the metal pot and you will scorch the bones." He is fidgeting with his napkin and I can tell that he isn't too comfortable talking about himself.

He turns to look at me. "Where would you like to go first?"

"Let's go see the facial reconstructions." I smile. We walk through the beautiful halls, first going to the human evolution, of course. We stop and stare at the skeletons of pre-humans and the creations that show how they might have looked. The center ceiling of the museum rises thirty feet to the top of the two levels, making it feel huge and open. The exhibits shoot off the main area, on two levels, and it would take an entire day to see everything, if not two. The floors are beautifully tiled in marble; the walls look like solid stone block. It is such an imposing structure, and its solidity always makes me feel relieved.

"There are your facial reconstructions," Mike says, nodding towards a *Homo erectus* skull and the face that was created beside it.

He smiles, and his deep-brown eyes hang on me. I blush with delight. "Yes, making exhibits looks like so much fun. I always wanted to do that, but got into forensics instead. But I still love museums." I give in to the glass eyes of the creature and admire the craftsmanship of the face.

Mike smiles at me. "I like your passion for the art. Very nice." He leans toward me, our shoulders touch, and I feel a thrill.

We explore the museum for a bit and then my stomach starts to grumble. "Do you like French food?" I ask.

"I like most food," Mike says.

The restaurant we are going to is a short walk from the museum. As we stroll by the other museums, we keep bumping into each other. I take that as a good sign. I guess this is a date. Good.

We walk by the Ronald Reagan Building, all very white and imposing starkness and stone. I choose one of my favorite restaurants for lunch: a French-bistro-style restaurant called Les Halles Cafe. I was there once and enjoyed the yummy French food, especially the profiteroles for dessert. The delicious puff pastry is filled with vanilla ice cream and then drizzled in liquid chocolate is my favorite. Yum.

The restaurant is unassuming from the outside, part of a corporate building, but upon entering you are transported to Paris. Dark wood-paneled ceilings, leather-cushioned seats, and mirrored walls create an image of being in a tasteful cottage in the Dordogne in southwestern France. We settle into a comfortable booth that faces onto the main dining area and the windows of the restaurant, a good people-watching position. Then we order drinks: iced tea for me, and a local beer for him.

"I'm curious, Mike: What is your office like? How do you macerate bodies there? I would love to hear your stories." Hearing my questions, I feel like a groupie, but I love to hear people's stories. Every office is unique, as different as each person in the way it is run, and the facilities it has. And I have always been fascinated by how the defleshing process is done. Once I saw a television show about how beetles are used to eat the flesh, but I don't know how they really do it. "What process do you use? I hear that warm water is the best way."

"I learned the steaming method when I was at Knoxville." He says this offhandedly, like it's no big deal. But it's a big deal to me. The University of Tennessee at Knoxville is one of the best forensic anthropology departments in the country. This is largely due to the Body Farm that was created by Dr. Bill Bass in the 1970s. I had considered pursuing my own degree there but ended up here instead.

"How long does it take?" I am fascinated.

"You can do an entire skeleton in about four to six hours from a partially fleshed state. It's not big enough to put an entire body in it, so we still will have to disarticulate it some. We wrap the remains in muslin cloth so we don't lose any small bones." He speaks completely at ease with his subject, and I feel gratified. The deeper I get into the field, the easier I find it to talk to people who are accustomed to death than those who are not. The food we ordered arrives, escargot to start then a tuna salad for him and a steak and pommes frites for me.

"You said that you spent some time here in D.C.," I prompt.

"Yes, I lived here in 1992. Things have changed a lot, especially after 9/11. When I first started working here, you could drive right up to the White House and walk unfettered around Lafayette Square. But the atmosphere changed in '95 after Timothy McVeigh attempted to blow up the Alfred P. Murrah Federal Building in Oklahoma City. After that the government got more and more paranoid, establishing more and more policies. They blocked off the road in front of the White House, put large cement barriers all around, metal detectors, more checks, et cetera." He gestures out the window. "You know how the landscaping is around the Washington Monument?"

"Not specifically," I admit.

"Well, the land around the monument is terraced, kind of like rice fields, to discourage vehicles from approaching it. Before that it was just sitting up there on a long sloping hill. Anyone could potentially drive right up to it. To prevent that they created the terraced system, reinforced by concrete block hidden underground at every level. Even the Walter Reed Army Medical Center campus posted guards at all the entrances." He sits back and sighs. "Things are a lot different than they were. We used to be a more trusting nation. The '90s is when people began to be uneasy, but after last year and the attacks that came on American soil, we've become paranoid and fearful. It's similar to the Red Scare of the '40 s and '50's."

I feel so ignorant about the many changes that have happened just in my own lifetime. My mind whirls in contemplating them all. The atmosphere of suspicion we live in now is in such stark contrast to my youth. As kids growing up in the 1980s and '90s, especially in upstate New York, we walked outside freely with no worries about kidnappers, and the worst thing that could happen on a plane was a hijacking, which was pretty rare.

"Why did you to get into forensic anthropology?" I ask while we share delicious dough-covered balls of ice cream.

He leans back and takes a sip of his coffee. I notice that he takes it black; very manly. "Well, when I was thirteen, my best friend Theo moved into an old house near me, in Kansas City, Missouri. We were playing in the attic; there was a lot of stuff left behind. There was this heavy old black chest, and when we opened it we found a skeleton. At first we thought it was some sort of Halloween decoration. But when we called his parents up, they were scared. They called the police, and it turned out it was a human skeleton."

"Really?" I ask, intrigued. "Whose was it?"

"Well, they didn't know for a long time." He smiles. "Eventually they found out that it was the child of someone who'd lived there before, and they passed away and their kids just sold the house with everything in it. The police had to find an anthropologist, and he was able to determine that there was no trauma to the body. So we don't really know what happened. But it did inspire me to become a forensic anthropologist. I always wanted to be able to find answers to unanswered questions."

"Wow, that is amazing." I breathe more slowly as he looks deeply into my eyes. His large brown eyes are large with long eyelashes remind me of cow eyes. I have a particular fondness for cows as I spent my summers in Brazil on a farm.

"What about you?" He leans toward me and takes my hand as it lies next to the water glass. His hand is warm and dry. "What made you want to be a forensic artist?"

"I don't have a story quite as interesting as yours." I move my fingers against his. Nice hands: muscular, tan and manly. "I have always been an artist; my mother and grandmother, too. But I was also fascinated by the origins of humankind and different cultures. My own cultural background is Japanese-Brazilian and Scotch-Irish, so there was a mix." I smile and look into his eyes.

"Yes, a very beautiful mix," he says, holding my gaze.

"Thank you." I tilt my head and blush. "I wanted to find a way to use my art, and initially was interested in becoming a museum artist. But then I found out about forensic art. So I've been pursuing it for the last several years and got my master's degree at George Washington and wrote my major paper about facial reconstruction. I wanted to go to University of Tennessee but was discouraged by my anthropology professor. Not enough jobs, he said."

Mike scowled. "Too bad that your teacher discouraged you. But I'm glad you're still using your passion. I saw the reconstruction you did. It was very nicely executed, well proportioned; it looked like a living person. A lot better than some I have seen." "I had a colleague whose reconstructions always had 'his' nose!"

"Well, thank you so much." I feel pleased and embarrassed. I still don't know how to take compliments well. "Yes, there is a large variation in the abilities of people who do forensic art. It really needs to be more professionally done. To effectively help people get identified and give their families some answers!"

"Yes, it is a big issue. I always want to help give people the truth."

After lunch I want to show Michael the National Building Museum. It is one of the lesser-known museums that I found a few years ago, and I love it. We meander east through the downtown streets, among the imposing and important-looking buildings to F Street, and then the National Law

Enforcement Officers Memorial, which is in front of the National Building Museum. It is an outdoor monument with a short wall that encircles the tiled clearing. On the walls are the names of the officers who died in the line of duty. At each corner sits two larger-than-life-size statues of reclining lions.

We cross the street into the National Building Museum. Michael opens the door for me and we enter into the huge open room that is the museum. The ceiling looked over a hundred feet tall with huge marble columns that stand at least five foot wide. The ceiling is constructed of glass so the building feels open, airy, and important.

We walk through a permanent exhibit, housed in a small room, on the history of Washington, D.C., architecture and city planning. I like to read all the information on the exhibit plaques. Fun facts are listed; like how Pierre L'Enfant designed the first planned city in the United States or that it was designated to be in the center of the country, which it was when the country consisted of only the east coast. That it was designated to be separate from any state, so it became part of the land from two states, Virginia and Maryland.

We talk nonstop, the conversation flowing easily. He tells me of his experiences, going to different mass disasters, pulling out bodies from airplanes and buildings. I am enthralled. The more time we spend together, the more I grow to like him, and the more attractive he is. I feel sad that he lives so far away.

"How long will you be in town?" I ask, fearing the answer.

"Until Wednesday. I'm here doing some research with colleagues and presenting on our recent NAGPRA activities."

My heart sinks at the short time he will be here but I don't want to sound that way. "What is NAGPRA?" There are so many acronyms in D.C., I can't keep up with them all.

"NAGRPA stands for the Native American Graves Protection and Repatriation Act that was signed into law by President Bush in the fall of 1990. A man named Mo Udall from Arizona originally proposed the act in July of 1990. This law requires that all public institutions, including museums and universities that receive federal money, perform an in-depth survey of any material holdings that might be of native origin. Meaning, all artifacts and, most importantly, skeletal remains must be documented and studied to determine their closet native group.

If human remains are determined to be Native American and can be traced via records or morphology to a modern group, then the institution must negotiate with the closest, or representative tribe will decide the appropriate next steps. Sometimes that means the bones are returned to the tribes for internment or, because of cultural sensitivities to the dead, schools or museums agree to curate them in perpetuity." He smiles and looks down, seemingly embarrassed.

"Sorry, I went into lecture mode." He blushes and I just like him even more. "It is a compelling issue for many institutions, and one I am passionate about. We see it a lot in New Mexico. We need to be mindful of where our study collections come from and under what circumstances they were acquired."

"I can tell you are very passionate about your work. That is really inspiring." I look at him and lean forward and kiss him lightly on the cheek. He blushes and pulls me in for a hug.

"I'm sorry I can't spend more time with you tonight," he says, "but I have to get back to prepare for my meeting tomorrow."

I deflate as I remember how short his visit is and how far away he lives. "I understand." I do, but don't want to cut the night short.

"How about we get together Tuesday night?" His eyes glisten.

"Sounds great." I perk up. At least I will get to see him again soon.

He walks me to the metro and we part ways. I head west to Virginia and he to his hotel in DC. Back at my home, I settle in with my pets. I really like Mike but don't want to, owing to distance. In my frustration I pull out a pad and do some sketching, which is always a good distraction.

CHAPTER 12

On Monday the bodies from over the weekend are being autopsied and everyone is busy in the back, but since Mary Lou is out, I have to stay up front answering the phones and performing office duties. I stay in the outer office in case anyone comes to the window. Funeral home employees sometimes come in needing of a copy of a death certificate, and once in a while, like Robert Greeley's wife, a family member of a decedent will show up. A few months ago, a couple came to the Medical Examiner's office to identify their son. We had already positively identified him through fingerprints, so we really didn't need their confirmation.

This morning it's quiet. Occasionally through the glass partition I see the building's door swing open, but this time people are headed to the forensic laboratory upstairs. The occasional officer looks over and waves at me, but most just walk by.

Part of my front office duties is going through the mail. There is a several-inch-tall stack of it, since today is the first day of the week. I page through each item slowly, reading it and putting it into the addressee's internal mailbox. It consists of mostly junk, fliers from restaurants, mail to the doctors, and some medical records pertaining to the decedents. Doctors' offices will usually fax those over, but sometimes a diligent nurse will also send a hard copy. In the middle of the pile, I come across an item for Patrick. It is a flier from the Fishersville High School alumni association asking him to join them for his thirty-year reunion. Fishersville. Hmm . . . The name niggles in the back of my brain. Where have I heard the name of this town before?

My mind is consumed with all the morning's work, so I shake my head and move on. When a person over forty starts losing their thoughts, it is often blamed on age, but I often have this happen. So what's my excuse? I figure it is just lack of focus. Trying to keep up with the many things that are going on is pretty challenging.

Mary Lou comes in an hour later, and I am able to go back to my office. Patrick is in the back assisting with the autopsies, so I have the room to myself. I move paper around my desk and come upon the file for Robert Greeley. That is where I heard the name Fishersville before. That's where Robert Greeley was from. I wonder if there's a connection. I pick up the phone to call Lisa and pause. She may not be up this early. I'll call her later.

My phone rings and I pick up. "Medical Examiner's office, Julia speaking, how can I help you?"

A man's voice comes through the phone. "Hey! This is Adam from the Western District office."

"Hey Adam. Is everything all right with the reconstruction?" I ask nervously.

"Even better than all right—great! We had an identification from your sculpture!" He sounds elated.

"I can't believe it!" I am humming with excitement.

"Yes, and we're having another press conference on Thursday. Can you come down for it?"

"I will have to ask my boss and see, but probably." I am excited and look forward to telling Michael Cuezze about the hit.

"Yes, he was identified by his cousin, then positively so with dental records she provided. I guess he had disappeared a while back, but he had some drug issues, anyway. But his cousin is very grateful. She saw the sculpture and is coming by on Thursday, as well. We would love to have you here."

Wow. My first reconstruction completed and a hit based on my work! I feel so glad to help the family get answers.

That evening after exercising at my apartment's gym I settle down to watch some brain-candy television. I remember that I wanted to call Lisa and tell her about the Fishersville connection, so I pick up the phone and dial her number.

After two rings her familiar greeting comes on the line. "Hey girl, what's up?"

"Guess what—my reconstruction was identified!" I say.

"Great! Congratulations!"

"I forgot to ask what his name was, but they want me to go back to Roanoke on Thursday for the press conference."

I then tell her about the reunion flier that Patrick received. "Did you find out anything about Robert Greeley's past? It seems like Patrick and Robert were the same age and he should know something about him, but he is being weird about it."

"Hmm. Interesting. I'm headed down to Steph's in Keswick, so not too far from Fishersville. I'll go there on my way back up and stop in at the PD on Friday and see if they have any insight." Lisa sounds distracted.

"I'll be driving back up from Roanoke on Friday. I'd like to go with you, if you're okay with that."

"Sounds good."

"Great, talk soon. Have a good night and tell Steph I said hello." I sign off.

CHAPTER 13

The next day at the office I wait until Patrick is out of the room and call Detective Francisco Garcia, hoping he will have more information for me about the robberies.

"Garcia." The slightly accented voice comes on almost immediately.

"Hey, good morning. It's Julia Rawson. I'm wondering if you came up with anything else about the case I discussed with you."

"Oh yeah, I was meaning to give you a call. I did get a chance to speak to my witness, the one who helped with the composite. Well, I showed him the picture, and he thought it could be the same guy."

I'm getting excited. "Can we talk sometime in person?" I want to do this without Patrick around, so am not sure what to do.

"Sounds good, I have to go back to the lab tomorrow, anyhow."

"Can we meet for lunch? I want to bounce some ideas off you. How about the Outback off Braddock Road at 11:30?"

"Sounds good."

I lean back in my seat. I want to ask him about Patrick and hear more about the cases that Robert Greeley went to prison for, too.

As I stand to leave the office, the phone rings and I answer it. "Medical Examiner's Office. Julia Rawson speaking."

"Hi, this is Investigator Dougin from the U.S. Parks Police. We got a skeletonized body out here in Great Falls Park."

As someone who minored in anthropology, I am always more fascinated by the skeletal cases than the fresh ones. Usually they are much less stinky, too.

"Sounds good. I'll come out for this one." I get the details of the location and put my bag together. As I am leaving, I stop to tell Dr. Reeves about the case. She is technically my supervisor and always treats me with respect, so I try to do the same to her. She is sitting in her office looking through the microscope at some slides from organ samples she had taken.

She looks up. "Let me know what you find." She turns back to her analysis but then looks up again. "Oh, by the way, I spoke to Dr. Marcosi, and I'm fine with you heading down to Roanoke again. Congratulations on the identification." She straightens and smiles.

"Thank you, it is very exciting!" I smile back.

Now I have not just one skeletal remains case but two. Too bad Michael Cuezze is busy today; I would love to have him with me to retrieve the body. I decide to take the van in case there is more of the decedent than just bone. I check the van to make sure we have clean body bags and other personal protective equipment.

I pull out onto Braddock Road heading east to Route 495 heading north—or west, technically. Route 495 is a huge circle that encapsulates the

Washington, D.C., area. It is over sixty miles of road, something I learned the hard way. When I first moved here, I missed my exit and figured I would come back around to it soon enough, as it is a circle. I didn't realize that it would take me an entire hour. So I always make sure I'm going in the correct direction on 495, which sometimes is difficult because the directions change depending where you are entering onto the road.

I exit onto the Georgetown Pike and drive northwest. It is a beautiful road with the Potomac River on one side and blooming woods on the other. My favorite view from this road is the towers of Georgetown University that peek over the trees on the other side of the river. They look so regal and inspiring.

The trees are bright green with blossoms in whites and pinks. The air is cool and crisp, a sunny, perfect day to be out.

The road weaves into Great Falls Park. At the entrance I let the park attendant know why I am there, so of course I don't have to pay the park entrance fee.

I approach the area that was cordoned off, park and hop out of the vehicle. A short man in a brown uniform is standing there waiting expectantly. He has a small, dark mustache and a serious expression.

"Good afternoon, ma'am. Investigator Dougin."

We shake hands. It feels funny to be called "ma'am" at my age. But I have learned that addressing a woman as "ma'am" is commonly taught in the South, so it doesn't necessarily mean that the speaker thinks you are old; it's just a polite way of greeting a woman you don't know or to whom some professional deference is required.

I follow him down the dirt path and then off it into the woods. "A hiker found this body," Dougin says. "Well, his dog did. The dog got off leash and wouldn't come back to the owner. The owner is pretty shaken up."

We approach the figure lying on its side next to a tree. It looks like the person just laid down to die.

The clothing left is a worn greenish-brown T-shirt and jeans. At the bottom of the body lie socks and worn brown shoes. The body may have been leaning against the tree when it still had skin, but without flesh to hold it up, it had fallen over onto its side. There are leaves around it and a small tangle of grayish, dirty hair near the skull.

Every step of the way, I take photographs, which will give the doctors a better idea of the scene and the body's position. I peer closer at the skull, trying to remember information from my biological anthropology classes. We learned how to tell the difference between a male and female skeleton and the differences between ancestral groups, or race.

The skull's brow line is stained from what I assume is decomposition fluid. There is a groove of bone over the eyes that protrude. That, along with the square jawline, indicates to my slightly trained eye that it is a male skull. The clothing supports this, but that is an unreliable source for judging a person's gender.

"It looks like a male to me." I squat down next to the body and pull on gloves. Then I insert my hands into the various pockets on the clothing. "Here's his identification." I pull out a Maryland driver's license with a man's face staring from it. It reads "Geoffrey Marks."

"Good." Inspector Dougin takes the license from my hand. He is standing on the other side of the body, examining the area around him. "We get these a lot. Somebody who is tired of living comes out to a peaceful place to end it. The National Park Service is the federal agency that gets the most dead bodies out of all the federal agencies."

I look up, surprised.

He nods, almost proud. "We have over four hundred national parks, where deaths are usually accidental and sometimes suicide. Only on occasion are they homicides." He frowns down at the body. "Well, I will still treat it as a homicide, just in case."

The body is held together by some dried skin and clothing. We comb the surrounding area in a ten-foot circle around the body, looking for the small bones of the hands and feet. There are 206 bones in the human body and most of those are in the hands, wrists, feet, and ankles. And although they may seem unimportant, they can actually tell a lot about defensive wounds and other health aspects of the person. I think of Michael and wish he were here, too. But I know he is busy. At least we will have something new to talk about at dinner tonight.

We find bones interspersed with leaf litter from last autumn, and I take photographs of each item in place, then with a scale next to it. I take more photographs than usual, as Investigator Dougin isn't taking any. I pause and look at my paperwork, trying to remember all the things I need to take note of and record.

I pull out a black body bag and a folded, clean white sheet. I unfold the sheet and tuck it under the remains and drag the body onto it, to preserve as much evidence as possible. When I pull the shirt taut, I see a cut through the front. I point to it. "This could be a stab wound. It's hard to tell, since the clothing is so dirty and worn. But it is suspicious."

Dougin frowns. "God, I hope not. That will complicate things."

I stand up and pull out my clipboard with my checklist for the death scene. I had missed noting the weather, something that does effect decomposition, but it is more significant for a recently dead body to estimate the time of death. "Oh, do you happen to know the ambient temperature?"

Investigator Dougin looks confused. "Not too sure right now."

"I'll check when I get back to the office." I will look at the national weather service and note the conditions for today and for the past few months. I still am not sure how quickly a body decomposes here. It all depends on the weather, temperature, humidity, and other aspects. I know I have a lot to learn, but I will definitely be asking Michael tonight.

Investigator Dougin helps me carry the body bag back to the van. We load it in and onto the table that is folded down on the floor, and strap the body so it doesn't move around. I notice a Great Falls Police Department car parked nearby to secure the scene. I guess Investigator Dougin won the jurisdictional issues. Sometimes, depending on the egos involved, police don't play well with one another.

I say good-bye to Investigator Dougin and then walk over to the Great Falls PD vehicle. The driver lowers the window as I approach. He's an officer I recognize but can't name. His nametag flashes in silver: "R. Canterbury."

"Ma'am," R. Canterbury says. He has a military-style haircut, short on the sides, slightly longer on top, and appears fit.

"Hey. We are taking the body back to the office and will look at it tomorrow."

He nods. "I didn't get the case so will just get the information from Investigator Dougin."

I shift my weight from one foot to the other, hesitant to ask my question. "I was wondering if you know anything about a string of robbery cases from several years ago." The fine lines around his eyes and stocky body makes me guess that he is about forty years old, so I am hoping he was on the force then. He looks at me blankly, then smiles and says, "We've had a few robberies since I've been here."

"Oh yeah, sorry, they were in Great Falls along the river and they got a guy, Greeley, for it." I forget how many cases they see over time.

He nods. "Yeah, yeah, I worked some of those cases, as far as I remember it seemed like a team of people hitting homes. But I don't think anyone was caught." He shakes his head. "Why do you ask?"

I sigh, a team of people. Interesting. "We might have a lead on someone who was arrested in Prince William and might be related."

"Great. Well, keep me informed." He takes out a business card and writes down his number. "This is my cell." He winks at me.

"Will do." I straighten up, not sure if he was hitting on me or not. He is wearing a wedding ring, but I have learned that for a lot of men being married doesn't mean anything.

I head back to the office with the small bag with the bones in it. On arriving I head back to Dr. Reeves's office. She is at her desk looking over her glasses at the computer screen. She looks up as I enter and say, "Just got back, I can't tell much from the state he is in, and there is a tentative identification from a driver's license that was on the body."

I update her as to the status of the case I just brought in. With a nod she says, "I'll take a look at it, but I would rather have a forensic anthropologist look at him, they have looked at more bones than I have. I heard Michael was in town this week, so when I was told this case was primarily skeletal I gave him a call. He is Metroing out in about an hour. Can you pick him up from the station?"

I flush. "That sounds good." I hadn't told her that Michael and I had gone out earlier. Foolishly, I didn't think it would come up. But they are old colleagues. I do not know if they are friends. The line is still hard for me to discern.

"Great." She readjusts in her chair. "I'm glad you came back to chat, I need to talk to you, anyway."

Uh-oh, I always get nervous when I hear that. "Am I in trouble?" I smile crookedly.

"No, no, not at all. I just found out that the main office wants to extend our investigation services. They want us to have an investigator available to police at all hours, so we are making your hours later, from 2:00 to 10:00. I don't know if you remember, but we talked about that possibility during your interview."

I nod, relieved and somewhat excited. The child in me is always afraid of doing something wrong and being admonished; some sort of residual fear of authority from school, or something. But it makes sense, now that each office has two investigators; they want to offer coverage longer. A lot of offices have investigators twenty-four hours a day, seven days a week, and I think that is what the Chief wants to achieve when we can. Progress, I guess.

"Okay, no problem. When do you want that to start?"

"Next week, after you get back from Roanoke. You can take the county car again." She smiles and looks at me over her glasses.

"Okay, will do, thank you."

I hurry back to my office to freshen up before I see Michael Cuezze again, even if it's for the last time. There my pessimistic tendencies show their ugly head. Why can't I just enjoy my life one moment at a time and not worry about the future so much?

I brush my hair out, refresh my face, and take the time to put on eyeliner and mascara. Michael is waiting at the curb at the "Kiss and Ride" of the Vienna Metro station. I think back to our kiss and hug the other night and smile.

I pull up to him in my Celica and lower the passenger window. "Hey, want a ride?" I call out.

He startles then smiles when he sees my face, and hops into the car. He puts his backpack at his feet and says, "I hear you got some bones for me."

"Yes, I just picked him up."

"Caroline wanted me to take a quick look. I was done with my meetings so had some time. I can at least verify the age and sex of the skeleton."

"Thank you so much for coming out. This is great—I'll get to see you in action."

"Looking at bones is not too exciting, but I'll try to make it so for you." He gives me a sidelong glance.

"I just heard that the facial reconstruction I did was positively identified," I blurt out.

"That's great!" He leans over and kisses me on the cheek before we start moving. "I'm impressed. I've never known of a reconstruction getting identified so quickly."

When we get to the office, I have him sign in and introduce him to the front office staff then takes him back to meet with Dr. Reeves. Then I head back to the morgue to pull out the new bones.

A few minutes later, Dr. Reeves brings Michael into the morgue. I have opened the body bag and have the skeleton ready for him to inspect. He and Dr. Reeves look at the remains. I hand them the photographs from the digital camera that I printed out.

"Nice photos." Michael smiles up at me from across the morgue table. He pulls on the latex gloves that are sitting on the tray. The skull is mostly bare and he picks it up slowly and gingerly examines each side. One by one he looks at all the bones I retrieved. I had laid them out in as much anatomical position as I could figure out. "Nicely done," he comments, but I notice that he moves a few of the ribs from one side to the other. Matt had already taken the X-rays, and they are pinned to the light board on the wall. The doctors walk over to it and switch on the light to illuminate the ghostly figure.

"There are a few healed fractures in the long bones," Michael says, pointing at the white leg bone image. "But they look old."

Dr. Reeves looks at the X-rays as well and nods. "I need to make a phone call—I'll be back in a few minutes."

Michael and I are left together in the morgue. I smile and chuckle at the strangeness of the situation. He looks good, wearing a blue cotton button-down shirt, with no tie. I can see the line of his neck muscle and collarbone. The tan skin and sexy arc of his muscles.

"Are we still on for tonight?" he asks.

"Absolutely." I smile. He smiles, too.

"I would love to hear what you see in the bones." I move to his side of the table. He proceeds to point out each bone, the arthritis in the vertebrae.

Dr. Reeves comes back in. "So you don't think it's a homicide?"

"I do not see any evidence of trauma so far," Michael says.

"I'm sorry that I can't spend more time with you," Dr. Reeves says. "I would have loved to, but I have plans for tonight. Maybe when you come back into town."

"Yes, of course. I would love to come back." Michael's eyes flick toward me.

"I'll make sure Dr. Cuezze gets to where he needs to go," I interject and try not to smile too broadly.

"Great, thank you," Dr. Reeves says. "I have to head out now."

I look at my watch and see that it is already 4:00.

"Oh yes, it looks like it's that time," I agree. We put the bones back into the morgue. "I was thinking about going to Old Town Alexandria," I say to Michael after Dr. Reeves is gone.

"Sounds good," he agrees.

I go into the bathroom and freshen up my lipstick. We pack up and head out in my Celica.

Old Town Alexandria is one of my favorite places in the region, with blocks upon blocks of historic architecture and quaint streets. It was settled even before Washington, D.C., on the mouth of the Potomac River as it heads out into Chesapeake Bay. The historic homes are tall Federal-style row houses made from brick or wood, perched along cobblestone streets.

I visit here often enough that I know the good places to park. Parking is free on the street, but usually hard to find. I am grateful for the parallel parking skills I learned in New York, and settle my darling Celica into a small spot. When we are parked, Michael leans over to kiss me on the lips. I smile and flush, glad that he is taking the lead. We walk up the street toward King Street, which is where many of the restaurants and shops sit. We have decided on a Spanish tapas restaurant that sometimes has flamenco dancing. I am not sure if they will have it tonight, but it is quite romantic.

As we walk up the hill to the restaurant, we pass shops selling locally handmade items, the town square, which has farmers markets in the summer, and then the area becomes more corporately commercial. Banana Republic and Starbucks have found their place nestled along the streets.

The sky is dark and the air has cooled down; a brisk spring air that makes me glad I'm wearing a scarf. But I am almost always cold, that is one reason I left New York – to get out of the cold. I am wearing my knee-high thick-soled boots that I picked up one year in Montreal. Those Canadians know how to make a boot to keep your feet warm. Michael takes my hand and pulls me to him. I snuggle closer to him and feel nervous and excited.

We go into the restaurant, and Michael looks around approvingly. The burnt orange colored walls are accented by dark trim, and a large painting of a bullfighter and a bull on the main wall are well done and spotlighted. "I like this. Very fun."

A small dark-haired woman leads us to our table in the corner. There doesn't seem to be live music tonight, which is good, as it will make talking easier.

We look over the menu and I order some *gambas aioli* and chicken with green sauce. And, of course, olives and Sangria.

Michael orders fish and vegetables. "I don't eat red meat," he admits. I am impressed; I have not met many men who are discerning in what they eat. "I just feel better not eating it, I don't mind if others do," he continues, almost seeming a little defensive of his choice.

"I think that is great." I smile and he relaxes, seeing that I am not critical of him.

He leans forward and rests his chin in his palm. I recount the story of the man who was identified in Roanoke and he is happy to listen. It feels nice to have someone to talk to about work issues, who doesn't get grossed out by issues concerning human remains and suspicious death. That is difficult to find. I have dated a few people, and after the initial "Oh, I watch detective shows," the intrigue wears off, and when faced with the facts of my work, they get repulsed. It almost made me feel like there was something wrong with me. So it's particularly nice being with a smart, handsome man who takes what I have to say as the norm. The thought of him leaving pushes into my head, and I shove it aside.

"How was your week?" I ask after I finish with my story.

"Oh, it was good. I had a few meetings with folks from the Smithsonian about how to take care of my Native American bone collection. And I got to have dinner with some of my fellow UT alumni."

"Sounds interesting," I say. We eat delicious food and finish off the bottle of wine. I don't want the night to end.

After dinner we walk down the hill toward the Potomac. It is a beautiful clear night, and I take his arm and it feels good. We walk in sync and just enjoy each other's company. Next to the water is a building that once was a torpedo factory. It is now an artists' co-op with studio space as well as shops for the public. It sits next to the boardwalk that is populated by benches, restaurants, and a pleasant green area. We walk by some of the small docked boats and settle on a bench. I lean against him and he puts his arm around me. We talk while darkness continues to descend. Fewer and fewer people are around, and we realize that it is almost midnight.

"I really do have an early flight back tomorrow," he says, and I note a bit of sadness in his voice.

"I-I . . ." I stammer, surprised to feel tears in my eyes. "I have really enjoyed our time together." I clear my throat, pushing the tears away.

He puts his hand on my cheek and kisses me gently. "I want to see you again." He hugs me close and nuzzling my ear he assures me, "This is not the end." Warmth washes over my chest and I exhale, relieved.

CHAPTER 14

The next day I feel sad knowing that Dr. Cuezze is flying back west, and I try to focus on work. I have my lunch meeting with Francisco Garcia, and I am looking forward to hearing what he has found out about the case. Patrick comes into the office and seems more relaxed. I am glad, as it's difficult to share an office with someone who is on edge and not in a good mood.

"So how is it going?" He stands near my desk and leans against the bookshelf that divides the office between my space and his.

"Oh, pretty well. Headed out to Roanoke tomorrow. I'm sure you heard they got a positive ID based on my reconstruction." I don't want to open up too much to Patrick. "How are you doing? Are you feeling better?"

"Oh. Congratulations." His eyes meet mine but they don't focus. "Yeah, thanks, better." He looks down and puts his hands together. "My wife, she's had a relapse. It's been hard."

I nod sympathetically although I cannot imagine what he is going through. Sometimes I feel bad for him, and sometimes I don't like him. It is a strange dynamic. I know it's hard for him to have me around, because he is no longer the one and only investigator so therefore he's less special. Plus I was never a sworn police officer and have a different mentality about life and the way things work, which makes it hard for us to relate.

"Who was the person identified as?" he asks.

"I think the guy's name was Joel Peterson."

Patrick freezes for a second, and then starts moving the papers on his desk. "I'm going back to see if Drew needs anything." He straightens his shoulders and leaves.

Okay. That was abrupt.

I work on paperwork, nothing out of the ordinary, until it's time to meet Francisco. The Outback Steakhouse is close by, and open only on Fridays for lunch. It is a regular spot for some of the lab people, but I hope not to see anyone I know this time, as I want to keep this newfound friend/source private.

When I arrive at the restaurant, Francisco is already there. I have noticed that many police officers like to arrive at their destination early. I think it's something that has been drilled into them, since they work in a job where they are relieving someone else and everyone likes to leave their shifts on time. Or perhaps it is because they are paid by the hour.

We settle into a booth in the back of the restaurant, with Francisco's back to the wall. Like the Mob, law enforcement people are always on watch for a predator. His eyes scan the room as we sit down before he relaxes and rests his gaze in my direction.

I smile. "All safe?"

He chuckles. "I guess you know the drill."

I nod. We look at the menu, to be ready when the server comes. Food always comes first in law enforcement. He puts the menu down and focuses on me. "I spoke to Lisa Byrd the other day, glad to hear that she's the one on this case—she's good."

"I'm curious about what you found out." We put our menus in a pile on the corner of the table.

"Well, a few things, it turns out, that seem pretty interesting. I met with the witness again; the one I did the composite with, to see what he could remember. He lived next door to one of the houses that were broken into during the robbery spree. He's a retired FBI guy and seemed happy to be helping out. He said that the guy that he saw during the robberies ran off when he saw the lights from his house come on."

I nod, nothing unusual there. "But," Francisco continues, "The interesting thing is that the witness thought he heard noises from the direction the suspect ran to. He described them as the sound of car doors slamming. That is, he heard *two* car doors, not just one."

A perky server appears to take our order. She is a young-looking blonde woman who seems happy to be there. I order an unsweetened iced tea, grilled chicken, and mashed potatoes—yum. Francisco orders a small steak with potatoes and a Diet Coke. We want to get our food orders in quickly since we are on a limited lunch break.

"So what do you think that means?" I want to hear his thought process before I voice my own. I am still trying to wrap my head around the scenario.

"Well, he could have opened a door to drop the stolen items in, but if he was in a hurry, I can't see someone doing that. Although it's not like criminals are all that smart. Or it could mean he was working with someone. Unfortunately we don't have any proof."

I lean back into the shiny blue seat. Another server delivers our drinks and asks if we need anything else. Francisco shakes his head and thanks her.

"Well, I got the police report from his arrest and the follow-up reports. There was no mention of him working with anyone, no known associates. But I did talk to an officer from Great Falls PD, who I came across at a scene, and asked him about it. He said they thought there was a team of people doing the robberies." He pauses with a smile. "So it sounds like there had to be at least two people. I looked up the case to see if anyone else was arrested for the same robbery, but nothing was attached."

I sigh. "Too bad. Maybe he had a vendetta with his old partner or pissed off someone else he may have come across. Is there any other way you can find out who his associates were? Or even if he had partners?"

Francisco nods. "I'll put out some feelers to the guys who worked the case, call in some favors, and touch base with some of the locals I know, too."

"Thank you. I talked to an Officer Canterbury if that helps. He gave me his card."

I smile as our food approaches. I can't wait to dig in. Plus food always seems to mellow people. We tuck in immediately.

"I am curious about something," I say after a few minutes of silent chewing. He looks up with a full mouth. "What do you know about Patrick McConnell, the other investigator at the ME?"

Francisco's jaw works as he finishes chewing his food, and then he dabs daintily at his mouth with the paper napkin, clearly thinking about what to say or, more accurately, what not to say.

"Well, I never worked with him myself, so I don't know firsthand."

I nod, intrigued, hoping he will continue. In an interviewing class I took, we were taught that it takes the average person seven seconds to respond to a question thoughtfully. Since then I have noticed how often people try to rush others or talk when the person being questioned is still trying to formulate their response.

"Are you close?" He raises an eyebrow.

I shake my head.

"Well, I don't know the details of why, but I do know there are a few people on the force who didn't like him. But he sure does seem to know how to grease the palms of the people who could get him whatever he wanted."

"Thank you for telling me. I have noticed that myself." I smile, thinking of how Patrick plays Dr. Deland so much. "So how long have you been doing composite sketches? I have done age progressions and facial reconstructions, but don't know much about composites."

"I've done about a hundred over the lasts two years. It's an interesting process. The department has been pretty supportive of me doing it on the side, but it always depends on who my supervisor is at the time." He keeps eating. "But I like to do the work, and it helps narrow down the field of suspects. I use the FBI reference book and let the witness choose the aspects of the heads that remind them of the suspect, then try to cobble something together."

We finish our meals over his composite sketch stories and put our credit cards down. Francisco waves to the server for the check.

I make it back to work in just an hour and five minutes. No one watches my time, but I want to be respectful of my coworkers and bosses, so I try not to take too long a lunch when I do leave. This time when I walk into the office, it's empty. I poke my head into the main administrative office and ask Mary Lou where Patrick is.

"I think he's in the back counting pills." She smiles at me. "You want some cookies? Please help me try to be good. One of the funeral homes brought them in." She holds up a plate displaying cookies that look like they are from the grocery store.

"Thanks, but no. I'm trying to be good, too." I smile back and slide into my office. Putting distance between the sweets and me helps my self-control. Not that I am a big dessert person, but sometimes I nibble when I am not hungry just because something is there.

I call Lisa and get her voice mail. I leave a message to call me back.

The red light of the voice mail is glowing at me, and I press the play button the message is from Justice Levi. "Hey Julia. I just wanted to say hello. And to let you know I'm happy to look at the photographs of the possible bike debris you mentioned. Let me know."

Oh yeah. I forgot. I take out the printed photographs and decide to go upstairs to his office. I call first to make sure he is around. He is, and I make my way to his office through the back stairwell.

He lets me into the lab through the back door, smiling. I smile back, "Thanks for taking the time to look at these." I look around, not seeing anyone else.

"Jason's off today." Justice says.

"Here are the photographs from that homicide from last week."

He examines the pictures. The first shows the inside of the Toyota's trunk. It was surprisingly empty, with just a crowbar and stained carpet with a pile of dirt in the corner.

The next photograph shows a close-up of the dirt. I could see it was clay—not surprising for Virginia, as most of the soil is red clay—and in a compact cross like shape.

"Hmm." Justice Levi takes out a magnifying glass for a closer look. "This definitely looks like a bicycle tire. Hold on."

He moves to his side of the desk and after a few minutes of rummaging, he pulls out a piece of paper. "This looks like debris from a mountain bike tire. It's hard to narrow down the brand for sure, but it could have come from the tread of a tire brand called Bontrager. They are owned by the bike company Trek." He hands me the paper with the image of the tire on it. "But I don't know if I could testify for sure."

I examine the picture of the tire. The knobs are square and spaced in a way that would leave dirt in the shape shown in the photograph from the trunk.

"Wow, thanks. That is amazing." I am impressed—knowledge always does that to me.

A prideful smile spreads across his face. "Well, I did a case about two years back with a bike. The suspect used it to flee and accidentally rode over blood from the victim. It left some interesting marks, plus the blood was on the tire."

"Thanks. I've got to go back downstairs. But I appreciate it." I step away from him.

"Let me know what you find."

"Will do, for sure. Thanks again."

I head downstairs with my thoughts whirling. What does this all mean?

CHAPTER 15

At 10:00 p.m. I am settled in front of the television watching *Law & Order*. I am practicing my people-drawing skills by sketching the character Jack McCoy, the lead prosecuting attorney from the show. I work to keep my drawing skills fast by trying to capture the fleeting image on the screen. I learned from Garcia that it's important for a composite artist to be able to draw quickly, so as not to make the witness wait too long.

There is a knock on the door and I pause, not expecting anyone. As a single woman I am always wary of late-night visitors. My gun, a SIG Sauer 232, is next to my bed, a room away. I don't know if I should bother to go get it not wanting to be overly paranoid. It's my personal gun, as I do not carry a firearm for my job. I learned to be comfortable with guns from a guy I dated when I was twenty-one, who introduced me to shooting. He first taught me to shoot with a .22 pistol, which I almost found fun. But when I shot a 9 mm, I was so unprepared for the power of the recoil that afterward I was shaken and upset by the potential damage that it could do. I definitely have a strong respect for firearms. At the same time I understand the feeling of safety one can provide for a female who lives alone. And, as I am learning more and more in my field, victims are usually women.

I walk to the entrance and peer through the peephole. Lisa is standing there, so I smile and quickly open the door and let her in.

"Hey! What's up? You want anything to eat?" Always my first question; she seems to eat all the time, but still manages to keep her athletic figure.

She shakes her head. "I got your message about Robert Greeley's ex-wife so I figured I would just stop by. I checked out her story. It does look like she couldn't have anything to do with it. She was with her family in Panama City Beach, and there's no trail in her financials of a flight up here." She walks over to my futon couch and sits down, looking comfortable in jeans, boots, and a black athletic jacket.

"She didn't seem the type to me, either—but what do I know?" I follow her to the couch. "I probably couldn't tell, anyway." I haven't honed my feminine intuition skills yet—or whatever you want to call them. Hopefully I will one day.

She agrees. "You never can tell with people. Anyway, remember I said I was going by the Staunton Police Department—the one that covers Fishersville? I didn't get a chance this time, but I will stop by next week. I did put in a call to the police department, though. I spoke to a senior officer who remembers Robert Greeley. He wasn't surprised that Greeley is dead. I guess he had been a troubled kid. His adult priors I already knew about, but I guess he had some juvenile arrests, too, that were expunged from the record. The officer suggested that I go by the high school and talk to the counselor, who apparently has been there forever and knows all; a Miss Anna Bell Mannon.

I'm stopping in there next week on my way back up."

"Hey, that will work out for me. I have to go to Roanoke and will be driving back around then. Can I meet you there and interview her with you?" I fill her in about the case for which I am being sent to do a reconstruction: a purported white male in his 50s, homicide victim with no identification, found in a ditch off the highway.

"Sounds good." She gets up to leave. "I'm exhausted. Call me when you're heading back from out west."

CHAPTER 16

Thursday I head back to Roanoke. I leave my beloved Celica at the office and take the county vehicle, a hideous, worn, gray Ford Taurus, loading it up with my reference books and equipment for the facial reconstruction as well as my own clothing. The car has no CD player, so I drive in silence rather than fight with the radio to find stations as I move in and out of range. I get on Route 61 heading west, and the hills on either side of the highway grow to mountains. The rise of the mountainside envelops me and my stress dissolves. I have been to the eastern part of Virginia, which is flat and swampy. This part of the state is almost the complete opposite. It is amazing how different each area of the state is.

As I go there are fewer and fewer cars on the roads and I pass more open space and trees. On Route 81 the traffic is mostly long-haul trucks, which I find intimidating to drive around. The route is pretty and I enjoy seeing new parts of the state.

In just over four hours I am pulling into town. I find the same hotel that the Western District office people have reserved for me—a worn-looking motel one near the interstate that looks a little sketchy. Hmmm. Ah well, it's just one night, then on the road and back home.

I unpack the toiletries and clothes I'll need tomorrow, knowing I will probably have to iron them, anyway. With a grumble, my stomach reminds me I haven't eaten and I drive around a bit searching for something interesting but give up and drive through McDonald's and pick up my dinner. I will do sit-ups when I get back to the hotel—on a towel, though, so I don't have to sit on the floor.

The next morning I get up early, dress in a black pantsuit (that I did indeed iron to make a good impression), and head to the office, a small brick building that looks new, at least newer than my office. I enter the door to the Medical Examiner's office on the first level. I see a sign for the forensic laboratory on the second floor, just like at my office.

The secretary is a blonde woman who looks to be in her fifties with hair teased high and hard-looking bangs. "It's good to see you again, Julia. Congratulations on the identification." She has a mountain accent local to the Blue Ridge, rather than the slow, quiet drawl I was getting used to in northern Virginia.

"Thank you so much." I smile and realize I have forgotten her name.

A few minutes pass and I examine the art in the lobby; uninspired prints of flowers probably purchased at a garage sale, which appear to have been haphazardly hung—the artist's eye.

Adam enters the room to let me in the back. "Thanks so much for coming back so soon." He leads me through the front doors, and as I put my bag down he turns to the door.

I nod to the ladies at the front door; I forgot their names already. Adam and I go into the back room, and there are coffee and doughnuts and even tea laid out. "Want some coffee?" Adam asks. I shake my head. I hate the stuff, even the smell. I know that makes me in the minority, but that is how I have always felt.

"Tea would be great." I sit down in the sterile break room, which has light-blue circular tables with hard metal-and-plastic chairs to sit on. "I would love to hear about this guy. Who is he?"

Adam puts a lot of creamer into his coffee and brings that and my tea over to sit across from me. "His name was Joel Peterson. He was a fifty-four-year-old white male. Apparently he has been missing for over seven years. His daughter just thought he left, took off, never to be seen again. Apparently her mother didn't have too many good things to say about him, and he had a bad habit of disappearing, mostly due to drugs." Adam goes on. "But when his daughter, Andrea, saw the reconstruction, she knew it was him immediately. She called our hotline and brought in his old dental records. He stops to sip his coffee.

"You will see Andrea today. She's coming by at 10:00 for the press conference. I think one of the reporters wants to talk to you first about the process."

Uh-oh. I never like being in the spotlight, but I guess for this it is a good reason.

After the conference it's time to "take him down" and make the sculpture back into a skull. The bones are evidence, and that fact can never be forgotten. It is now my job to remove all the clay without damaging the skull to put it back with the rest of the body in case his family does come forward and wants to give him a proper burial.

In the back room, I work with gloved hands to remove the soft matter—slowly and carefully pulling off pieces, moving methodically to avoid damaging the delicate facial bones. Once I get the clay off, it's time to take off the tissue depth markers and glue that stayed on. I use a swab dipped in acetone to remove the bits of adhesive that are encrusted to the skull. Everything is thrown into a biohazard bin for safe disposal.

I cautiously remove the mandible from the skull and swaddle them in bubble wrap then carefully place them into a cardboard box. After everything is in, I push the lid down and slide packing tape across the box to secure it, and then delicately add red evidence tape to the box. To show that I closed it and I am done with my analysis, I scribble my initials and the date across the tape with a Sharpie marker. Chain of custody maintained. Done. I pack up my belongings and say my farewells to the staff at the Western District office. It has been fun to see how things are done here. I head to the hotel to get a good night's sleep.

CHAPTER 17

The next morning I wake up glad to be heading home. I have some tea and pack up my few belongings and take everything out to the car. During my absence, a pet sitter came by to visit the cats, but I know they will be happy to see me when I get back. Contrary to a lot of people's beliefs, my cats do miss me and are very affectionate—and not just for food. I miss their little faces, too, as well as being in my own apartment rather than in a mediocre hotel eating fast food.

I get into the county car and head north on Route 81. I had seen the Fishersville sign on the way down and knew that I should get there around 10:00 a.m. After a quiet few hours with not too much traffic through the rolling hills, I pull into the small town of Fishersville. There are only two main streets, so I explore the first street and luckily find the high school on the right-hand side. It is a sprawling brick building that was probably new back in the 1960s.

Lisa's police car is already parked in the lot, and I pull up beside it. I get out, a little stiff from the drive and week's work, and stretch my legs before ambling over to her window. She lowers the window and looks like a typical cop with her sunglasses at the tip of her nose. The only thing missing is her hat. She says it is uncomfortable to wear—especially while driving.

"Hey," she says. "I just came from the police station. They didn't tell me much, just what I pulled from their records. Everyone on the force is too new to know any gossip from that time."

"Well, let's hope that Miss Anna Bell Mannon will remember something. Did you give her a heads-up?"

Lisa shakes her head. "Nope. I wanted the element of surprise. I'm interested to see the authentic expressions on her face when I bring up Robert Greeley. It makes it easier for me to tell if she is being honest."

We head into the school, and Lisa in uniform gets attention and interested looks from everyone who sees us. As we stride down the hallway together, I feel very official—she in her uniform and me in my black suit.

We head to the door labeled "Main Office," which opens with a ring from a cowbell attached to the interior handle. A heavyset woman sitting behind a desk looks up in surprise. "Can I help you?" Her Virginia accent has a different sound then those I heard in Roanoke, reminding me of Scarlett O'Hara in *Gone With the Wind.*

"We are looking for Anna Bell Mannon." Lisa towers over all of us in the office and looks especially imposing in her uniform, even without the hat.

"Oh, well, I hope she's not in any trouble," the woman says, looking confused.

"Not at all, ma'am. We just want to ask her some questions about students from a long time ago."

"Well, she will know all about that, then. Third door down on the left."

Lisa and I make our way down the halls that seem too low, lined with thin yellow-colored lockers that are no taller than I am. We find the door with the letters "Guidance Counselor" taped onto the glass portion of the door. The "S" is peeling off.

The door is partially open, and Lisa knocks as she pushes in. The small woman seated in the office has a halo of wispy white hair, a kind face, and twinkling blue eyes.

"Miss Mannon?" Lisa asks, holding her hat.

"Can I help you?" Her accent is a genteel Southern one, smooth like butter. There are so many different types of southern accents. Her office is dark and cozy, filled with books and photographs. On the floor is a worn blue-and-black rug that appears to be handmade.

"Yes, ma'am. I am Officer Lisa Byrd with the State Police, and this is Investigator Julia Rawson." She gestures toward me. "May we ask you a few questions about some of your former students?"

I chime in, "Miss Mannon, I've just come from Roanoke, where I was working with your nephew, Adam, ma'am. He says hello."

I look to my right and see a miniature rocking chair with Raggedy Ann and Andy sitting in it. Their unblinking eyes stare at us; it's a bit unsettling.

"Oh, Adam—he is such a sweet boy." She leans back and appears to relax. "Please call me Miss Anna Bell, everyone does. I'll help if I can. Please have a seat."

Lisa and I sit down in the small chairs in front of Miss Anna Bell's desk, and Lisa starts.

"We are here investigating a death that involves a former student of yours. Robert Greeley." Lisa pauses but there is no change on the counselor's face. "I don't know if you remember him, since it has been almost thirty-five years since he graduated." Miss Anna Bell's face is still but her eyes squint in thought. I can see the gears in her head moving.

She swivels her chair around to face the bookshelves next to her. She runs her thin and gnarled finger along the spines of the book. Each is dark green with the year emblazoned in gold. "That would make him class of 1967, if my math is still right."

I have to use my fingers to calculate that. She is sharp.

"Yes ma'am," I say.

She pulls a book from the third shelf. "Greeley, Greeley." Her finger indicates a black-and-white face looking out at the viewer. She turns the book for us to see. The young man is wearing his hair long, in a ponytail, with sideburns and a surprisingly full dark mustache. I can see the eyes and the head shape from the driver's license and body that I picked up.

"Oh yes, I remember Robert Greeley." She leans back in her chair, nestling into her thick wool sweater even though it feels warm to me in the room. "Such a sad story. Like so many, he came from a broken family and his dad had a drinking problem. His mom died when he was about thirteen or so, and his dad drank more, then either ignored or beat the kids." She shakes her head.

"I am sure you were a great help to him." This is my attempt at creating a bond.

"Oh, I don't know. He only came in to see me after his mom died, but then he got more and more angry and disillusioned with authority, like boys do, especially those growing up in the 1960s. It was a crazy time—the escalating war in Vietnam, the Summer of Love, and all that. He started to hang out with the wrong crowd, or, rather, a particular boy, and they got in some local trouble." She looks off to her left, as though viewing her memories on a mental screen.

"What was his name? Oh yes, Patrick something with an M . . . McConnell. That's right, yes, McConnell."

I feel the blood drain from my face.

"I didn't see any accomplices in his police record." Lisa speaks slowly, and I can see she is just as nervous as I am.

Miss Anna Bell leans forward conspiratorially. "Well, Patrick was always such a spoiled boy. He got away with every bad thing he did on account of his father, who was the pastor at the town church. The town was even smaller then, and everyone really knew everyone else. There was another boy, an older boy, who was a bit slow, who they let hang around them. But they were quite mean to him. I think his name was Joel Peterson." She leans back. "I heard he left town a while ago. I never knew what happened to him."

I had stopped breathing. "I know what happened to him," I croak.

She looks up, surprised. "How would you know that, dear?"

"I just came back from working with your nephew at the morgue in Roanoke. We identified a body that was found. It's him—Joel Peterson."

Miss Anna Bell looks down and leans back into her chair. "That is sad. So many sad stories over the years."

I feel like my brain is on overload with thoughts running through it. What does this mean? What are the implications? What do I do?

"Thank you, ma'am, for that. Was there anything else?"

Thank goodness Lisa has the ability to remain focused on the task at hand. Miss Anna Bell goes on a bit longer, but it all just sounds like noise to me. All I can hear is the blood rushing through my ears as I think of Patrick—my partner—Patrick.

Lisa and I do what we can to extricate ourselves from the guidance office with a flurry of "thank yous." Neither of us can speak as we walk out of the building, each digesting the possibilities of this new information.

"Food?" Lisa breaks the silence once we get outside. I smile. Cops never forget a meal. It is about lunchtime, and we do need sustenance to think.

"I saw a pizza place on the main street," I say. I, too, am always on the lookout for food I like. We head to the Pizza Palace, a small restaurant on Main Street with maybe twenty tables, each covered in the ubiquitously Italian-American red-and-white checkerboard tablecloths.

A "Please Seat Yourself" sign greets us at the door. We find a table situated away from the few other people in the establishment—of course Lisa has her back to the wall.

"Wow," I open. "This is not good."

"That's what I think," Lisa agrees.

A young woman with dark hair in a ponytail ambles over to take our order. We had agreed on a cheese pizza to share, although I know Lisa would have preferred some fun toppings. I just like cheese, with red peppers and garlic. Yum.

"So what do you think this means?" I address the elephant in the room.

"Well, none of the implications are good. Did you ask Patrick about this case at all? Did he tell you that he knew Greeley?" She adjusts her utility belt, trying to get comfortable.

"No, I think he was off that day." I pause to think back. "I don't remember talking to him about it at all."

Lisa shakes her head. "I was so tired from the intensity of the reconstruction and out of it, but I don't remember him being at the autopsy. Was he there."

I think back. "No," I try to recall what happened that day. "I think he was off that day."

We stop to eat. I am surprised to see how delicious looking the pizza is, being in rural Virginia, which is not known for the largest Italian population, when it arrives on a metal pedestal. I reach for the crushed red pepper and salt parked at the end of the table—a necessity for pizza in my opinion. Lisa takes two pieces on her plate and I do the same. We munch in silence.

"Yeah, I think I did ask him about the robberies later, but not that case specifically. He said he didn't remember them. What a liar."

"Well, it does seem pretty sketchy to me. The fact that he didn't mention that he knew Greeley. He had to have seen him on the paperwork, right?" Lisa looks up at me.

"I would think so, even if he was off that day."

We continue to nosh, not knowing what to say. The pizza might absorb the acid that is forming in my stomach.

"Try to find out what you can from him," Lisa folds her last piece of pizza in half and shoves it into her mouth and seems satisfied. We split the bill and head out the door.

"I'll see what I can do. See you back in Burke," I say when we are standing at my car.

She has to go to another State Police office on the way back to northern Virginia, so she gets in her car and heads eastward through the grassy mountains.

I drive back with thoughts of Patrick swirling in my head. What did he do? How much is he involved? I drive slowly up the highway, passing the rolling hills dotted with cows and other livestock amid historic wooden barns in various states of decay or use. A landscape I do find serene, very similar to the one I grew up with in the rural areas Saratoga county, New York.

I take my time to make sure that I get back to the office after Patrick has gone. It is 4:30 when I pull into the office parking lot and notice that only Dr. Reeves's car is there. I sigh with relief. I park and unload my personal bag into my own car and take two trips to unload my work materials from the facial reconstruction into the office. I am amazed at how much stuff I actually brought. On my way out, I stop into Dr. Reeves's office and report on how the facial reconstruction went.

"Great to hear." She is wearing her running gear already, a blue tank top with a black sport bra peeking out from under it, and black running leggings, showing her muscular and fit figure. "I got a call from Dr. Marcosi and he said that you did a great job. It was pretty quiet here—I've got to go—meeting a friend for a run." She stands and smiles at me; her smile is a rare and welcome sight. She is never unpleasant, just not a very demonstrative person and always so serious and intent on her work. "Don't forget that you start the new schedule next week. 2:00 to 10:00."

Oh yeah. I had almost forgotten. I feel relieved, as my new schedule will give me space from Patrick to think without distraction. I will overlap him for only two hours.

When I get home the cats yell at me, making me feel a tinge of guilt for having left them. But I feel so relieved to be home, and that it's the weekend and I have no obligations. I feed the cats then unpack my bags. Simon and Kudo are easily mollified by a fresh can of food, clean water, and fresh litter box. As I watch TV to zone out from the day, my black fuzz ball, Kudo, jumps onto my lap and purrs. I am forgiven.

I try to put all the ideas about Patrick out of my mind, but I still toss and turn through the night. The cats are upset that I am not staying still, and they abandon their usual places on the bed sometime in the night. But they come back bright and early when it is feeding time. I manage to give them a can of food and then roll back into bed. I am happy that I don't have to get up so early.

CHAPTER 18

Over the weekend I clean the house, and occupy myself between my art, mindless television, cooking, and sleep. It feels good to just rest on my own; the week was more strenuous than I realized at the time. As a confirmed introvert (I took the Myers-Briggs Type Indicator test and am an INFP, which stands for introversion, intuition, feeling, perception), I find being around other people energy zapping. Monday morning comes and my body and cats are confused, as I sleep to 9:00 a.m. because I don't start work until 2:00. But as always, it feels good to sleep.

As soon as I get to the office, I jump into helping in the morgue, which is swarming with people wandering around the space. There are several police officers watching, as well as all three of the doctors working on bodies. I push myself into the fray and help wherever I can. I keep my eye on Patrick, where he is busy at Dr. Deland's table, as if I could divine his guilt from just looking at him.

Later that afternoon the chaos dies down, and Patrick and I are in our office together. I feel anxious and unsure how to act.

"What did you go back for again?" he asks, still sitting at his desk. I can see the top of his head over the bookshelf that acts as an imaginary border between our areas.

"We had an identification of the body." I watch his back closely. "They identified him as Joel Peterson."

Patrick stops his movement. "That's great." He clears his throat.

I walk over to his desk, and my eyes drop to a framed photograph sitting on the shelf behind him. I freeze. I hadn't noticed the photo before, or remembered the details. It shows Patrick and two other men posing in the woods, each perched on a mountain bike smiling at the camera through their sunglasses. They are clad in serious multicolored biking shorts, gloves, and helmets. I had known Patrick was athletic but didn't know that he mountain biked as well. My heart starts to thud as I notice the brand of bike: Trek. Patrick stops and looks behind him at what I am so obviously staring at. "What?" he asks.

"I haven't noticed that picture before. I'm looking at going for a ride. Where are the best trails?" I ask, not having any idea of what else to say.

"Oh." Patrick seems to relax. "That was taken down in Great Falls Park; they have a bunch of trails there. From easy to harder."

"Cool, thanks." I step back to my desk, to hide my face with the barrier and screw up all the courage that I have.

Then I say: "I was working on that case, Robert Greeley. I just found out he grew up in Fishersville." I try to sound nonchalant. "The other day I noticed you got a card from Fishersville High School, so I was wondering if you knew him."

I don't hear anything immediately from over the bookshelf and am afraid to move. Patrick clears his throat. "Yeah, I might have known him. I think he was in my high school or something. I don't really remember, it was a long time ago." Patrick stands and glares at me, his face hard. "When John called he said you were headed to Fishersville. You know that's not your job. That's for police. You're not a cop."

"I know. I was with Lisa, though." I am caught between defending myself and being mad that he is bossing me around.

"Did you find anything?" He glares at me.

"No. It was just a hunch she had." My breathing is shallow. How could you possibly forget the guy who was your best friend, even if it was thirty years ago? He is lying.

Patrick looks at his watch. "I've got to go." He switches off his computer without shutting it down, grabs his bag, and strides out of the room. I gasp and start to breathe again.

Wow, asking him anything was a bad idea. I turn to focus on my computer and think about something else. It is impossible, though, and I just stare at the same e-mail for minutes.

I shake my head and look at my notes from the cases that I still have to finish reports on. Dr. Deland has already gone for the day, and I hear the back door open and close around 5:00. I assume it is Dr. Ivanovic. He doesn't always remember I am here, and his social skills are such that he doesn't always say hello or good-bye. I have learned not to take it personally. Dr. Reeves left earlier; she jogs religiously after work. So now I am alone.

Being alone in the morgue is an odd, eerie feeling. I am already on edge with the news about

Patrick. I don't want to think the worst, but the whole situation is questionable. The air-conditioning kicks on, and the noise almost makes me yelp.

I put a CD into my computer to make my own noise and quell my imagination.

Prince's voice comes out the computer's small speakers and I start to relax.

The phone rings and I jump at the unexpected sound. I turn down my music and pick up the receiver.

"Hey girl." Lisa's voice is light and cheery. I smile, relieved. "Want some dinner?" she asks.

"Yeah, definitely." My relief spreads through me at the thought of having her here. "I feel like I shouldn't leave the office, though. Would you mind bringing food in?"

"How does pho sound?" Vietnamese pho soup is a light and delightful meal, and maybe it will help calm my nerves.

"Perfect. You know me—can you get the one with just the regular steak? I don't like all of the other stuff, the tripe and such. I'll give you money when you get here." Yay. Pho! I have been introduced to so many delicious foods since moving to the D.C. area, and the Vietnamese broth is one of my favorites.

"Yeah, I know—you are a wuss." She laughs; she is much more adventuresome and usually gets the soup with tripe. Yuck. "Did you find anything on Patrick?" she asks. "I've put some feelers out about him. But his being an ex-cop, I have to treat this lightly."

"I'm sure we can talk about it when you get here."

"I'll be there in a bit." She hangs up.

I force myself to get lost in the paperwork in front of me—cases assigned by the doctors from today's bodies. Dr. Reeves asked me to get some further background information on a case of a sixty-two-year old while male that was found in bed and had no doctor of record to sign the death certificate. It looks like I will have to track down his family and his status about his health. Luckily the next of kin is listed. This makes it easier, but never a fun call.

The phone rings again. "Medical Examiner's office, can I help you?" I try to sound official.

Lisa's voice comes through the line. "It's me. I'm outside."

I let her in the back door. Two plastic bags carrying our delicious fare weigh her down. She is wearing jeans and a sweatshirt but still has her police boots on.

"I've got to go to the bathroom and want to heat up the food. Not at the same time." She chuckles. "Did you find anything in Patrick's desk?"

"I haven't looked; I wasn't sure if I should."

"Sure, why not? There's no expectation of privacy at work, anyway. Nothing illegal about it," she assures me. "We are just looking. I'll be right back."

Lisa heads off down the hall and around the corner to the break room. I want to be by the phone in case anyone calls, so I stay in my office while I wait for Lisa and dinner. My curiosity is piqued about Patrick. The thought of going through his desk flitters into my mind, but I feel weird doing it. But, hey, why not; opportunity knocks.

His desk is calling out to me to take a look. I don't know what I am afraid of, finding something or not finding anything at all. Why would Patrick kill this guy, even if he did know him? Why would he pretend he didn't remember him? So many questions.

I step around the bookshelf, walk behind his desk, and pull open his top drawer; pens, pencils, tacks, some gum and miscellaneous business cards—the usual business essentials. I don't really know what I am looking for. The next drawer is bigger and has more office supplies and a metal hip replacement. He had told me that he'd taken it from a body for training purposes as an example of how surgical implants can help identify a person. The manufacturer can trace the identification through the serial number stamped on it to the facility they sold it to and ultimately the implant recipient.

It is made of titanium in an odd and heavy shape. It has a ball on one end that fits into the socket joint of the hip, and on the other end is a sharp point. The point is driven into the femur to replace the piece that is sawed off. It is sharp and weighs at least twenty-one pounds. I start to replace it in the drawer and notice a small Post-it Note that was under it.

On the yellow note there is a phone number scribbled down: 703-555-1752. Hmmm . . . that seems familiar. I remember that it's Robert

Greeley's sister's number. I recall it since the numbers are the same as my childhood home's number with just a different area code. My heart is already racing yet I feel cold.

"What are you doing?" Patrick's voice rings through the room. I startle and let out a yelp. Patrick is standing in the doorway, his face dark.

"I—I'm just looking for a marker." Wow, that sounds lame even to me. "What are you doing here, anyway?" He's not supposed to be in until tomorrow morning.

"I forgot something and needed it." He charges at me and stops just inches away. "You weren't looking for a marker."

Fear surges through me but I am starting to get pissed. "I thought that you didn't remember Robert Greeley."

"What the hell are you talking about?"

I pull out the Post-it Note from his desk. "This is his sister's phone number!"

"Screw you." He turns around, flustered, grabbing the chair in front of his desk and slamming it down. His face drains of any emotion and his features turn into a mask. He takes a few steps around the desk toward me, and I see the menace in his expression. I scream and push the desk's rolling chair toward him. He stumbles in the small space. Then I see him reaching for the titanium prosthetic hip I left on his desk.

Designed to be driven into bone, it is as heavy as a hammer and as sharp as an ice pick. I don't want to be on the receiving end of that. I huddle in the corner and look around for what I can grab to defend myself.

"Hey! Stop!" Lisa's police voice booms from the other side of the low bookshelf, and her pistol is pointed at Patrick.

He grabs me and bends his arm around my neck, his strong arm squeezing me. He swivels me between him and Lisa, pulling me close as a barrier.

"Goddamn you!" Patrick yells in desperation. "I had no choice. I couldn't let him take me down, too. My family needs me!"

"What about Joel Peterson?" Lisa yells. I reach my hands out trying to grab something. There is a lot more to the story than I can think of right now. But I can't think at all. I can feel his body shaking and his arm tightening around my neck. My mind is a blank. He is focused on me and Lisa. As my arm reaches down, I feel my fingers touch the metal prosthetic. It feels like a slow mental process, but it takes a split second. *My coworker is trying to kill me. I pull the metal ball end of the prosthetic into my hand and hold it tight. Gasping as he tightens his grip around my throat, I thrust the sharp end behind me, into Patrick's flesh.*

He screams out as the metal goes into his leg and he loosens his grip. I drop my weight to the ground, trying to scramble away.

The sound of the gun going off is deafening without ear protection. Patrick falls back and I scramble toward Lisa on my hands and knees.

She bends down and pulls me to my feet then pushes me behind her, keeping the gun pointed at him. My ears are buzzing from the gunshot, and I can only faintly hear moaning. There is blood all around me and I crawl through it, slippery on the tile. Lisa holds her gun on him and with her free hand points to me then to her bag that she dropped at the doorway. She is saying something to me. "Handcuffs." Her voice sounds small and low through the roar of the blood through my ears. I scrabble through her canvas tote and find her handcuffs. I bring them to her and she proceeds to cuff his hands together in front of him while he is lying on the floor. Then I see her pick up the phone.

I am in a daze watching her watch him. Through the daze I hear banging at the front door. Lisa points and I go to the door, and see a group of people peering through the glass window into the area. I open the secured entry and they rush into the building in unison.

Uniformed police officers swarm in, pausing at me. They search my hands and look around the room for a weapon. I sit down like a rag doll, letting them frisk me, as I am unable to understand what they are saying with my ringing ears.

An older dark-haired officer stays with me, confused about whether I am a problem or a victim.

There is more swarming and Lisa is pointing and shouting. Then two people wearing scrubs come in with a gurney. After several minutes I see Patrick rolled out of the building. His hands are still together in the handcuffs, but his arms are bent as he clutches his right shoulder. I know Lisa is a good shot so she must not have wanted to kill him.

The officer who is with me leads me to his patrol car. I get a ride in the back, feeling more and more in trouble. The officer eyes me in the rearview mirror as I look at him through the cage. I still can't quite hear. Presently I am led into a small interrogation room. I have never been in one before. The walls are lined with thick foam padding, the noise-reduction kind, I think, my mind observing like this is all a television show.

The adrenaline seeps out of my body as I sit alone in the room. After what seems like forever, Detective Nguyen strolls in—he must be the lead investigator. We have met before at the morgue; I remember liking him then. I am not so sure now.

"So tell me what happened." His voice sounds like it is coming through a tunnel.

I pause, not knowing where to start, and then recite the events starting with Robert Greeley. When I finish he asks me again.

I relay the story again, knowing this is procedure. It still pisses me off, though. He leaves the room after what feels like hours, and I put my head down on the table.

I wake when the door bangs open. This time Lisa, Detective Nguyen, and Detective Francisco Garcia come through the door. I could jump for joy upon seeing Lisa but don't think that would be appropriate.

Detective Nguyen speaks first. "Well, you are free to go." He smiles for the first time today and his brown eyes twinkle.

"Let's go." Lisa puts her arm around me. "You will need to change." She hands me a bag with a black, long-sleeved shirt that smells like she keeps it in her car. I look down and see the blood stains on my grey shirt. In the bathroom I look at myself in the mirror, surprised to see that I am still there. There is blood spray on my neck that I didn't wipe away. I wash my face and put on the clean shirt, luckily my pants are black to hide the evidence.

When I come out I see Francisco, confused. "What are you doing here?" I still have no idea what is going on.

"Let's go for a drink. I think you need it," he says and leads me out. Lisa follows us and gets into her own car. She is wearing a white t-shirt and jeans and has removed all evidence of being a police officer, and looks surprisingly normal.

I drive with Francisco to the closest bar and Lisa pulls in behind us. We don't speak until we are all in a booth and have ordered drinks.

"What is going on?" I look from Lisa to Francisco.

Lisa begins. "We found out that the Great Falls PD guys suspected that Patrick was part of the robberies that happened seven years ago. They thought he was feeding information to Robert."

"How?" I ask. "What?"

Francisco takes over. "Well, you know how people sometimes call the police to let them know they're going out of town and to have patrol keep an eye on their house?" I nod. "Apparently he was feeding Robert that information so he could plan to break in. Then if there was a call, Patrick would respond and not do anything."

He grins happily when the drinks arrive and takes a long sip of his rum and Coke, or a Cuba

Libre. I take a swig of my vodka tonic. It feels good sliding down my throat, cold and bitter. The alcohol strips the stress from my body as it washes down me.

"Anyway, the connection that you guys found brought it together." He gestures at Lisa. "With that info they got a search warrant for Patrick's house and found money with Greeley's fingerprints on it. They pulled Patrick's phone records and found that he had indeed called Greeley's sister house from his home on at least two occasions. I suspect that he got a disposable phone after that." He leans back in the booth. "Oh yeah, and they found the Trek bike. It looks like the same dirt from the trunk is on his tires. So we suspect that he met Greeley somewhere he rode to, then bludgeoned him and put his bicycle in the trunk to set up the scene to look like an accident. I guess he was hoping to get some lazy police officer who would just call it in as a traffic accident and not get an autopsy. Not you two meddling kids." He chuckles at his Scooby-Doo reference. "Who knows?"

"What about Joel Peterson?" I ask.

Lisa leans forward, holding a beer bottle. "We're still looking into that, but I did ask a friend of mine and they found out that Joel had been visiting Robert in jail over the last two years. Then it stopped."

"Maybe they were trying to blackmail Patrick together," I suggest.

"Yes, Joel was a bit slow, working as a janitor in a school in Richmond. I don't think he would have come up with anything on his own. Robert must have told him to approach Patrick."

"Too bad for him," I say and lean back. The female server brings over food that I don't remember ordering. My forgotten hunger suddenly rears its head, reminding me to eat, probably because of the booze and the cessation of fear, a slow release of tension from all the muscles in my body.

"Patrick has been having financial troubles with his wife and son's health problems," Lisa continues. "We suspect that Greeley was threatening to give him up to the cops. We looked at Patrick's financials, and he has been depositing funds to Robert's ex-wife for the last seven years. $1,500 a month. We think that was the deal with Greeley, which Patrick pays for Greeley's kids' support and Greeley keeps his mouth shut about Patrick's involvement. That's not a lot of money around here, but it's definitely something, especially on a government salary."

She pauses and we take another sip of our drinks, absorbing it all.

"Wow. You guys are awesome." I lift my glass to them and lean back against the seat, letting the alcohol take the stress away. "Especially you, Lisa. Thanks for saving my life."

We clink glasses and each take a long swig. Francisco laughs. "I never liked that guy, anyway."

Epilogue

I had two weeks of forced sick leave and spent some of it in New Mexico. Dr. Michael Cuezze invited me out for a visit, and I took him up on it. I found a cat sitter and left my worries in Virginia. Michael offered me his guest room, and I knew he was a gentleman. But being in his comforting embrace led from one thing to another. Now that I am back in Virginia, I miss the smell of him on me.

I had to go back to work, and the atmosphere in the office has changed dramatically, as one might expect. I look at people with a more cautious eye. People are rarely as they seem.

I heard that Patrick is going to take a plea, since the forensic laboratory found trace evidence of soil and fibers from the car on his mountain bike. They also found a tiny bit of blood on the bike's handlebar. Patrick should have paid more attention in his forensics training, and not just left it all up to the Crime Scene Unit. The lab report said the blood belonged to Greeley. Like I said, gloves, gloves, and gloves. Locard's exchange principle never fails.

There is a budget crunch going on in the state now, and there have been rumors of jobs being cut. The Department of Motor Vehicles office has already announced closings. I am told that I am safe, but one can never be sure of the future— something I have learned in the last few weeks, for sure. Although people in the private sector have told me a government job is secure for life, I am learning that this, too, is a misperception. There are a lot of those. You just never know.

Thank you for joining Julia Rawson on her adventure. If you enjoyed it here is what you can do next:

If you liked the book and have a moment, I would appreciate a short review at Amazon.com (Amazon purchase is not necessary). Also, share the book with your friends - your help in spreading the word helps tremendously.

You can also like me at facebook.com/catyanaskoryfalsetti, follow me on twitter @catyanafalsetti and check out my webpage for my blog and more at www.catyanaskoryfalsetti.com. Thank you so much for your support.

ABOUT THE AUTHOR

Catyana Skory Falsetti was born in Sao Paulo, Brazil to a Japanese-Brazilian mother and Irish-American father and grew up in Saratoga County, New York.

She is a graduate of the State University of New York at New Paltz and George Washington University, where she earned her master's degree in forensic science.

Falsetti has worked in several roles, including forensic artist, crime scene investigator and death investigator for various law enforcement agencies throughout her career. These include the Prince William County Police Department in Northern Virginia, the Office of the Chief Medical Examiner in Northern Virginia, the Harris County Medical Examiner's Office in Houston, Texas and the Broward County Sheriff's Office in Ft. Lauderdale, Florida. She is also a member of the American Academy of Forensic Sciences.

Currently, Falsetti lives in Phoenix, Arizona, with her husband and their cats.

32773397R10119

Made in the USA
Middletown, DE
17 June 2016